CW01662856

DESPITE ALL ODDS

C. A. LADITAN

All rights reserved. No part of this publication may be reproduced in any form without written permission from Tiara Publishing LTD.

Copyright © 2022

Christiana Ayodele Laditan

ISBN: 978-1-8383255-7-2

DEDICATION

This book is dedicated to my father Late Mr Ebenezer Oladunni Shaw JP and my mother Late Chief Mrs Caroline Awele Shaw JP for bringing me into this world and all the impact they have made in my life including helping me to become a strong independent woman.

CONTENTS

ACKNOWLEDGMENTS

I would like to thank the following people.
My dear husband for encouraging me to write this book. Tayo Popoola for his assistance. My daughter Mrs Osinloye for her support and Mary Badmus for helping to proof read.

CHAPTER ONE

Born in 1952 at Osogbo in Osun State in Nigeria. I attended different primary schools; Holy Child, Grange School Ikeja and Staff School Ibadan. Gained admission to Queens School, Ede that later moved to Ibadan, which was one of the best schools as at that time. Queens school was owned by the old Western Region in Nigeria on about 20 to 22 acres of land. The motto of the school was and still is Pass on the Torch. Teachers at Queens school were very dedicated and committed. Housemistresses were very strict but caring and loving. They imbibed a lot of discipline into us including how to sit, walk and keep quiet when eating in the dining hall. On completion of my West African examination, I moved to Olivet Heights Oyo for my A levels.

Queens school was an all-girls school but it

was totally different. Olivet Heights was a mixed school for boys and girls. As you drive into Oyo township from Ibadan Olivet Heights is on the right-hand side on about 20 acres of land. Surrounded by such beautiful flowers and bungalows all cream in colour. An obvious chapel right in the middle with a big cross on the very top. Your first point of contact was the senior house master, Mr. Oluokun. Registration is completed in front of his little but modern bungalow, after which you are located to a house. Olivet Heights was full of experience as they had students from different secondary schools coming in for A-levels. Late Rev Lafimihan was the Principal. He was a strict man, disciplined but caring. May his soul rest in peace. Students were afraid of him and you dared not enter into his bad books, otherwise you are in big trouble. Late Rev Lafimihan had many years of experience; he was one of those veterans who had taught most of the students' fathers before they were born at all. It was therefore easy and a habit for him to identify students by their names and say 'I taught your father when he was in school.' Students were generally scared of him. Two years at

Olivet Heights were years of my education I would never forget. When the bell rang for breakfast, lunch or supper, students would jump through the windows and grab their food bowls. Once you were late, there'd be no food for you. Unlike Queens, there were no queues before going into the dinning or prayers before eating. Nothing like sitting down and eating together like civilized students. I just could not understand but it was typical of a mixed school. Thus, I came out of Olivet Heights, Oyo a very tough and strong woman.

I was in Atanda house, which was perhaps the worst house in the school. At least most of the bad boys in the school came from Atanda house. As for why I was put in Atanda house, I do not know. Queens school on the other hand was totally different. Students were well behaved, well cultured. We were taught to obey the bell, remain silent when eating in the dinning, queue up properly and obey school rules. There was time for everything every single day. Students treated one another with respect. Seniors were also strict but kind. We looked up to prefects as though they were gods. You wouldn't dare mess around with them. I was in Baobab house and I always felt it was the best house. Casuarina they said was full of ladies. The third house was Palm house but not as prominent as Baobab and Casuarina.

One of my fondest memories at Queens School is of my Yoruba teacher Mr. Popoola. He disliked me and some of my colleagues with a passion because we bore English names like Williams, Shaw, Coker, Johnson, Hastrup, Peters, Thomas, Moore and Richards. Every time he came to class, the first thing he would say was that all the students who bore English names should go out and once we could tell him the meaning of our fathers' names, he would let us in. He would always say our fathers were slaves of the white people. We would then stand in front of the class begging and promising him that by the next lesson, we would have gotten in touch with our parents to give us the meaning of our names. Only then would he let us into the class. Dare one of us ask any question, he would say "Yes, *eru oyinbo.*" This translated means "the white man's slaves." The whole class would then burst into laughter. I personally enjoyed his high sense of humour. Sometimes, he would call one of us to explain to the class where we originated from. Once you mentioned your state, he would say *"omo eru"* sit down. He was an original Yoruba man with genuine Yoruba idiomatic expressions. Sometimes he would come up with proverbs in Yoruba and tell us to explain the meaning of each one. Obviously, some of us would just write anything, which gave him the opportunity to say that we are not real Nigerians.

Oh, my music teacher popularly known as Mama Laoye. She was a woman who had so much passion for music. She loved the piano. The piano was her central entertainment piece. For her the piano was a true joy. The piano in the assembly hall was classy and always shinning. Mama Laoye made sure it was polished nearly every day. She made us understand that playing piano with singing is good for the brain and functioning of the entire body. She also used the piano to present students with real live entertainment which always made us look forward to her music lesson. Her favorite song was "I like to see a woodpecker, always by my side "Her legs were always on the piano pedal, she would move her head constantly from left to right and right to left laughing constantly. She played with so much confidence alongside melodious, mesmerising, spellbinding and delightful songs we listened to after she was done with the main lesson.

The Medical room was also like a ward in a real hospital. Once you knew you'd landed trouble with a senior, all you had to do was fake an illness and head to the Sickbay. Pretend you are sick, the nurse would admit you and there's every possibility that once you were discharged you would escape the punishment from the seniors. As you come through the wide door of the medical room the nurse would shout. "what is your name ? Your house? Your class? Nature of sickness? After which she would put the thermometer under your armpit. The funny thing is she would then put her glasses on and spend about 2 minutes checking your temperature, after which she will announce your temperature loudly. While taking your temperature you are constantly praying that she should not send you back that there's nothing wrong with you. Although she hardly sends anyone away because she wants to make sure that students are well cared for.

Seniors were looked up to as small gods. It was not bullying but there was just something special about all of them. The way they spoke to us in front of the dinning or assembly hall was always articulate. They had the ability to speak fluently and coherently. Whenever they came on stage to address us they commanded so much respect. Their uniforms were always well starched and ironed. White blouses immaculate. I remember the likes of Dora Chizie, Funmi Osoba and Kofo Ogunshola. Senior Kofo was tall beautiful and smart. She really knew how to walk with long strides, shoulders high and an excellent command of English. Seniors took pains in ironing their uniforms. They were much admired by junior students. Queens school girls were queens prepared for future generation of Nigerians.

Resumption at Queens School Ede was something students in general looked forward to. Most students came from Ibadan as transportation then was very easy, safe and interesting. Some parents would personally drop their children off in school, while majority of the students would take the Train from Ibadan. It was always packed full from Dugbe railway station Ibadan to Ede, despite the train's final stop being Oshogbo. Once the train was about to start its journey, the station master blew the whistle and we would all pop our heads out to wave to our parents who stood patiently to see the train move with a loud noise of *fakafuku faka fofofo*.

On the other hand, travelling back to Olivet heights Oyo was totally different. I never looked forward to going back to school. In fact, three days before resumption I would start panicking. On resumption day, you would take public transport from Ogunpa motor park Ibadan, students faces all screwed up. Within two weeks, all provisions packed in heavy suitcases on resumption would have disappeared; a massive difference between Queens school Ede and Olivet Heights Oyo. However, the experience of both schools remains a memorabilia.

After completing my A levels at Olivet Heights, I got a job at Atakumosa high school Osu which was very close to Ilesha. There, I taught for nine months. At the time, it was easy to get a Job in the Western Region prior to your going to University.

The name of the Principal was Late Chief Fashoranti and former governor of old Ondo state in Nigeria. He was a father figure during my stay at Atakumosa. One notable thing about Atakumosa was the special Bean cake called *Akara Osu*; massive in size but very oily and filling. You could eat one and not eat for the rest of the day.

Travelers travelling through Osu always found time to stop and buy the bean cakes. Long queues of cars and public transports were an indication that people really enjoyed eating the bean cakes. The place was referred to as Acara Osu depot. After nine months, I left Atakumosa high school with the intention of gaining admission to University. Unfortunately, I was unable to gain admission. I decided to stay at Ibadan which was close to home and teach at Baptist grammar school Idishin Eleyele. I taught for one year and was the housemistress for the girls in the School. The Principal was Late Mr Popoola. Who hailed from Ilaro Yewa Local government. I enjoyed my role as housemistress especially the pranks students played after lights out in the evenings. It was a memorable experience as well. After leaving Baptist Grammar School, I sought admission into university again but it did not happen.

My father tried his possible best to ensure I gain admission into one of the universities in Nigeria. At some point, I was given a letter to the Vice Chancellor of the University of Ibadan. On getting there; I was told that it was too late. I was given another letter to the University of Lagos but the story was the same. My dad decided to try for the last time and got a letter from Late Mr Dotun Oyewole, our next-door neighbour in Lagos. The letter was to the Vice Chancellor of Ahmadu Bello University Zaria. My mum travelled with me to Ahmadu Bello University Zaria which is in the northern part of Nigeria by train. It was a tedious journey to Zaria. The journey gave us the opportunity to see the different parts of northern Nigeria. I was astonished to see some the inhabitants of Manbilia Plateau walking half naked and using leaves to cover their body from the waist downwards. After two days on the train, we finally arrived in Zaria. University of Zaria looked exactly like University of Lagos from the main entrance to the administrative block. Looking back, the Nigerian government had put a lot of effort into education then. Unfortunately, I couldn't accept the course I was offered which was to do with religious education. I sought for admission in different universities but was turned down because I was not qualified for the course of my choice. At this point, the future looked bleak and uncertain. My dad was now very solicitous.

Sitting in front of our house at Ibadan one Friday afternoon, I sighted my mother coming home earlier than expected from her supermarket. She owned a big supermarket on the main road called Caro stores. Caro stores was stacked full of different provisions but we dare not go near the supermarket. When in need of stuff for the house we would go to other stores. She always wanted to account for every penny in her supermarket stores. Usually, mum left home at 9am and would not return round about 7pm. We all played our little pranks between 10am and 6pm every day. The house was always noisy, with all of us shouting arguing, cooking different things like frying plantain, frying yam, making chin chin or other snacks. Eyes were always on the clock. Once its 6pm we start cleaning the house and putting things back in place because of my super mum otherwise we will be in hot soup if she finds the house in a mess. The absence of my mum at home is an indication that the house is free for all. I therefore wondered why she was home early. She smiled at me as I tried to collect her bag. My mum was not a woman who would smile except something out of the ordinary had happened. She was a strict, rigid and stern woman who had no time for sentiments, someone you didn't want to mess around with. When she prepared food in the kitchen, it was compulsory for all of us to line up until she was done with cooking. Visitors were not allowed in the house and we were not allowed to go out as well, except times we sneak out when she was not around. She would also take us to the market in turns so we could see how she shopped for the house including comparing prices and how to buy good quality food without wasting money. Mum was a very good driver, after shopping she will ask us to start plucking pepper in the car so once we get home, we start cleaning the peppers and tomatoes.

Getting inside the house, she sat down and

informed me that she had met one of my old teachers from Queens School; Mrs. Banjo who'd asked after me. She said she informed her I was still at home trying to gain admission into a university in Nigeria. Mum said Mrs. Banjo suggested I attend an interview the following week to be conducted by Western Region Ministry of Education for Scholarship to study abroad. And if I was interested, I should attend with all my credentials. A ray of hope in sight! I surely did not want to raise my hopes yet having suffered disappointments so many times in the past.

I gathered all my credentials the following week and found myself sitting in front of a panel of highly placed educationists in Ibadan Western Region. After a hectic interview which lasted for about 5 hours I was told that I had been awarded a scholarship by Western Region to study B.ED Home Economics at any university of my choice in the UK. I left the ministry so elated and enraptured at the sudden turnaround in my life. On getting home, I realized that all my credentials were not with me including the letter for my scholarship. I'd left them inside the taxi I took from the venue to the house. I became so agitated and dithery, ran back to the junction where the taxi dropped me off but did not see the taxi or the driver. My tears of joy turned into tears of frustration. I had to drag my legs back home because they were no more functioning properly. My throat was dry and my head pounding as if mum was pounding yam inside a mortar. My tummy had this growling, gurgling noise and people passing by could hear the rumbling in my stomach. My temperature was high, could feel the hotness in my body without having malaria.

What would my parents say? How would they receive the news that all the evidence of my education had disappeared? School certificate, A level certificate, testimonial, and birth certificate. Breaking the good and bad news was what I dreaded most. As my dad came in, he asked about my interview. I quickly replied "good sir." I allowed him to settle down, took off his shoes before I knelt down to relay the good news followed by the bad news.

My dad was furious. He yelled and started calling me names. Flooded with tears, my whole world had crumbled and my heart was broken. My dad was quick to inform me that I would need to apply for the job of a house help since I didn't have any credentials to show for admission into any institution of learning. I went to bed without eating and woke up the next morning with a feeling of emptiness. Depression was creeping in there was this sense of loss of purpose, feeling of rejection and all-round anxiety. What next? My situation looked hopeless and defeatist. Mum was quick to support my dad in lashing words at me. There was no sympathy from anyone. When dad reprimands mum must support whatever, he says. My dad had visitors that week and on arrival of every visitor, he was quick to tell them that my education had come to a standstill because I lost all my credentials. All felt sorry for me while some made suggestions on how I could get the media involved so I could retrieve my documents. All suggestions made fell on deaf ears as my parents were no longer interested. Sleepless nights and waking up with so much uncertainty. My whole world looked empty and I could see it crumbling.

After five days of absolute misery, there was a knock on the front door. It was our next-door neighbour. He informed me that my name was mentioned on the government local radio called Rediffusion. They had reported that one Miss Ayodele Shaw forgot her credentials in a taxi and the taxi driver had dropped all the documents at Mapo Hall. Mapo Hall is the Colonial style of building at Ibadan city hall on top of Mapo Hill in Ibadan Oyo state. Mapo Hall was commissioned during the colonial era by Captain Ross in 1929. It is said that no political rally is complete without a stop at Mapo Hall. I realized instantly that Gods plan will actualize. I dressed up and quickly took a cab to Mapo Hall where I had to sign for the documents before they were handed over to me. One statement the man uttered was that I would definitely be great in life because the taxi driver had waited patiently for two hours outside Mapo Hall for officials to resume before coming in to hand over the credentials. God had shown himself strong in my life. He wanted me to travel abroad. Now, I was sure that I would be travelling to the United Kingdom.

There were massive forms to fill from the ministry of Education. Dad and myself spent endless nights filling forms for the ministry of Education. The following week I applied to different universities in the UK. Eventually I got admission into four universities but my dad settled for FL Calder University of Liverpool L18 3JJ. Dad had travelled to UK twice in the past so he could remember vividly places of interest that he felt would be beneficial to me in my choice of school. I had tried getting into different universities in Nigeria but to no avail. Now, four universities offered me a place to study BED Home Economics." God said at the appointed time, he will perfect all things concerning you".

Right from childhood, I have always wanted to be a teacher. During Christmas holidays, I would gather children from our neighborhood and organize Christmas carols while serving them snacks and drinks. I would invite parents in the area as well. This I did for four years consecutively. Interestingly, I would now be leaving for the UK to be a teacher in future.

Dad and I moved to Lagos in preparation for my journey to UK. The preparation was an interesting experience. My dad, out of excitement decided to do all my shopping himself. From suitcases to tights, socks, jumpers, jeans, tops, underwear and winter coat.

Few days to my travelling, dad took me to Lagos to buy the little bits and pieces left. Getting to Balogun which is in the heart of Lagos market, the driver parked at the back of a big shoe shop called Bata. Bata was a very big outlet for selling quality shoes with many outlets in capital cities and suburbs. Bata shoes were the best and could be rated equally with Clark shoes in the UK.

Just as my dad was about to cross the road to the other side without looking right, a big commercial bus colloquially known as *"MOLUE" Locally built public transport"* on top speed nearly hit him. I screamed "Daddy! Daddy!"

God in His mercy did not want to put me to shame. What if the worse had happened? Definitely I would not be able to travel. What would people say? Guilt will haunt me for the rest of my life if anything had happened to my dad. God made sure that the plans He had for me was not hindered. Getting home, I noticed my dad did not mention the incident to my mum and I kept it to myself as well. Dad found time to explain about his two visits to UK by boat. How long it took them to get to London, and all the different places he visited with my mum. His story about the UK made me excited and I looked forward to going to London. It wasn't until I returned from the UK that I managed to tell my mum about the incident that happened in Lagos when my dad was nearly hit by Molue. She was in shock. I then told her that at least nothing happened to my dad and I was back from the UK as a graduate. She laughed and said "Praise God."

Finally, the day arrived for me to travel to the UK. I had never been to the airport. My parents, maternal grandfather, boyfriend, boyfriend's dad and brothers were at the airport to see me off. It was an early morning flight, Nigerian airway from Lagos to London Heathrow Airport. Just as I was ready to board, my dad pulled me back and gave me a stern warning. Dad looked adamant and unrelenting. He said to me, "Make sure you face your studies and don't let me down. Don't get pregnant. Wait till you complete your education and come back to Nigeria before you get married."

"Yes sir" I replied, before heading into the plane. I knelt down to say farewell to my grandad, father in-law and mum. Then straight into the plane. With my dad, Education was the key.

Throughout the journey I could not eat out of excitement. Looking through the window, I saw mountain tops, hills, sometimes water, and at intervals, houses. I kept thinking about what my father said before boarding the plane. I dared not let him down, otherwise I'd be dead. Although he was a very strict dad, I loved him. He was tall, handsome and highly educated with excellent choice of English words. Why would I hurt him? No way! Dad loved all his children and he wanted the best for us all.

The plane landed at precisely 5pm. At last, I made it to the United Kingdom. *Could it be true?* I pondered inside me. I went through immigration including health checks being a new student. Everywhere was clean, sparkling with specific directions on where to go. So you couldn't miss your way. This took some time and as I came out, I ran into the arms of my aunty, Mrs Tola Imoiko. I'd never met her but as I sighted her, instinct told me she was the one. And sure enough, she had a card with my name boldly written on it. She had come with her husband to pick me up.

On our way home, I was flabbergasted with what I saw. Street lights everywhere, cars moved freely, no rushing, no reckless driving, no beeping. All roads were tarred and traffic lights everywhere. Everyone obeyed the traffic lights. You would think it was early in the morning and not in the evening. On arrival at my aunt's house in Brixton, she asked about my impression of London based on what I had seen so far since my arrival. I told her that it was something I could not explain as I was still in a state of shock at what I had seen. I was served Jollof rice with chicken and fried plantain with a nice cup of hot tea; quite a filling meal. It was more than satisfying, really delicious. I felt at home in her house during my five days stay. I was opportune to go shopping with her at Brixton market where I saw lots of Jamaicans. Sunday morning, I took a train from Euston station to Liverpool. This gave me the opportunity to see farm lands, factories and small cottages.

CHAPTER TWO

As I came out of the station struggling with my suitcases, I saw someone carrying a placard with my full name written on it. I introduced myself and she gave me a handshake. Her spoken English was totally different from the English I was used to. She asked about my journey from Nigeria and also my journey from London to Liverpool. I really struggled to understand what she was saying. Some of the things I did not understand but I had to smile as if I understood her. We both headed for a taxi waiting to convey us to school. On arrival, my heart was beating fast. It dawned on me that my journey as a student in the UK was about to start. I looked right and left but could not see someone of my own colour. Within two hours, I completed my registration, after which I was introduced to the Principal, Mr. Kenworthy and the lecturers. I was later taken to my hall of residence. My room was very clean with built-in wardrobe and medium sized bed. There was a small sink in the corner of the room. I unpacked all my clothes, shoes at the bottom bit of the wardrobe and finally my toiletries in the bedside cabinet next to my bed. After settling down, I broke down in tears. How come I had not seen any black student? I asked myself if I was in the right place. One thing I was sure of is that I couldn't go back to Nigeria at least for now. After unpacking, I changed into my night dress, knelt down, said my prayers and fell asleep.

A knock on the door woke me up the next day only to realize it was morning and time for breakfast. I rushed to the bathroom, had a quick shower, got dressed and headed for the dining hall following the directions. It was in the dining hall that I first noticed that I was on a journey of absolute loneliness. I sat down for breakfast and looked around, only to realize once again that I was still the only black student. Everyone seemed to be looking at

me. Was there something wrong with me?
The only black student in this massive hall?
It was a full English breakfast, eggs sunny side up, bacon, sausage, mushrooms and baked beans. Every table had a toast rack with toast bread. After struggling to eat, I stood up and headed for my room to get ready for briefing. Thank God I knew the right way to use a fork and a knife and putting them together after eating. My mum had always taught us table manners right from when we were young. These lessons included use of teacups for drinking tea, not using teaspoon to drink tea, sipping tea nicely without any noise, quietness while eating and pushing your chair in after food. So, I was able to fit in easily and no one would make fun of me.

In the main hall, old and new students and lecturers were discussing freely. Just as I came in, the Principal Mr. Kenworthy walked up to me and said "Hi Christiana. Did you have a nice night?" I nodded with a smile. At least his English was very clear. He had a very pleasant, soft hearted and warm personality and was more of a father figure. He actually asked after my dad and mum and I thought this was so sweet of him. Mr. Kenworthy informed me that I would be having a mentor who would support me during my first year.

Induction of new students started the third day, after which lectures started. All new students were taken round the school and shown the main common room, administrative block, dining hall, Food department, Textile department and home management building, laundry room and hall of residence common room. I was beginning to feel lonely and I missed home terribly. During lectures, I struggled with the accent. It was more of *Liverpodian* language. So, I had to pay serious attention in class to be able to grasp my lectures as Lecturers were always too fast when talking

After the first week, I was sitting in the common on a Friday afternoon when a lady, Melanie Bernette came towards me. She sat down and asked after my name and where I came from. Melanie told me she was from Northern Ireland. She had noticed me sitting all by myself throughout the week. When I told her I was from Nigeria, she asked, where Nigeria was to which I replied "West Africa." She told me she wanted us to be friends because she was lonely as well. We became very good friends, in fact inseparable for the three years I spent at FL Calder. Initially, I struggled with her Irish accent but eventually we fully understood each other. I always felt at ease with Melanie. She was a loyal friend till the end. Melanie was a friend you would call "secret keeper" We attended lectures together, went shopping together including Pubs on Saturdays. The first time we went to the Pub, I felt so uncomfortable as I'd never been to a Pub before. In Nigeria, people usually say "Beer Parlor." While Melanie would order for alcohol, I would order a non-alcoholic drink. Sometimes, we would go for karaoke night. Karaoke is a form of entertainment, offered by bars and clubs, in which people take turns to sing popular songs into a microphone over prerecorded backing tracks. Wherever I went I was conscious of the fact that I could not afford to let my father down. I did not want to get drunk like the many people I had seen on the streets. My background did not permit such.

When my dad called from Nigeria, he knew from my voice that I was not happy. I made it clear to him that I was extremely lonely and missed home seriously. He made me understand that I was not in Liverpool to make friends but to face my studies. Dad forgot it was more of a psychological thing. Not having your family and friends around you could be very traumatic and chilling experience. To be fair, most of my Lecturers were helpful but my mates did not make me feel wanted in any way because of the colour of my skin. Every time students were in the common room waiting to attend the next lecture, no one would sit next to me. The only time I felt comfortable was when Melanie was around me.

A month after my arrival in Liverpool, I decided to go shopping in company of Melanie. Our destination was the shopping mall inside the city. What happened will remain a memento in my life. We got on the bus going to the city Centre from L18 3JJ. There was no oyster card then so I paid for my bus fare. The driver had to give me the extra change. He made a lot of effort dropping the coins in my hand, careful enough to avoid any physical contact with my hands. As if that was not enough, no one sat next to me. Melanie had got in first so she just sat with someone on the front seat. Did it bother me? No. I was beginning to develop a thick skin now. There was nothing wrong with me. God made different colours and different people so life can be interesting. It made me remember this song "In Christ there is no east or west , in him no south or north. But one great fellowship of love throughout the whole wide earth"

Getting to the city Centre, I was amazed at what I saw; quite a number of black people. We also went to a place called Granby Street and I was quick to ask a black shop owner why there were black people in Granby and none around my university. The Granby Street area is among the oldest multicultural neighborhoods in the country, due to immigration following post war period. She explained that there was a big dockyard in Granby Street and most of them were sailors. I was able to buy some Nigerian snacks for a change. From then on, I would occasionally go to Granby Street, as it gave me a sense of belonging anytime I saw people of my own colour.

Buses were not very regular on that side of Liverpool. One Saturday morning, I decided as usual to go shopping at Granby Street. I had to wait for about 30 minutes at the bus stop. While waiting for the bus, I noticed a couple with their daughter of about 13 years old also waiting for the bus. The husband gave me a fake smile and asked, "Where are you from?" I answered politely "Nigeria." The wife went further to say "Oh! I remember I watched a program about Nigeria some years ago." She went further to say that people were poor in Nigeria and people lived in slums and mud huts. I replied nicely by telling her I did not come from the slums and that my parents have a beautiful house in Lagos which was then the capital of Nigeria. I told her most people live in luxurious and baronial houses in Nigeria. Their daughter out of curiosity went further to ask why I was so different from them. I replied saying, "There's no difference, your skin is white and mine is black. I was created by the same person that created your dad and mum. We all came into this world the same way and we will all die and be buried the same way." Whether she understood what I said or not, I couldn't care less. The dad replied, "This is true you know" in a typical Liverpool accent. Her mum then chipped in, "What brings you to this area?"

"I'm studying at FL Calder" I replied.

She replied "Really?"

"You must be really intelligent to have come all the way from Africa to study in Liverpool."

"Yes" I replied.

The bus eventually came and we all went in. As usual, I sat alone. After four stops, they got down and the woman said to me "see you soon". I felt good about the answers I had given them.

Eating in the dinning was my worse night mare. I missed eating my nice hot spicy Nigerian foods. There was no *Eba, Jollof rice, Amala* with *ewedu* or *Ila*, Pounded yam with *Egusi* soup or *Efo riro*, *Ogbono*. There was no yam or *Moinmoin/Akara* with *Ogi* or Eko, yam pottage and so many others.

Every time I walked into the dinning; I would ask the dinner ladies "What's for dinner?" The menu had been clearly stated on the board outside the dining but I would intentionally not look there. Some of the menus I could remember where Spaghetti Bolognese, Shepherd's pie, Kedgeree, Bangers and mash, Fish and chips with mushy peas every Friday.

There was also Chicken casserole, Liver risotto, Roast beef with roast potatoes, assorted vegetables and so on. There was always vegetarian choice for every dinner. I actually loved the desserts or perhaps puddings. The likes of Pineapple upside down, Apple pie, Apple crumble, Rhubarb crumble, Eves pudding, Bread and butter pudding, Lemon pudding, banana pudding, rice pudding, semolina pudding and so many others. Apple crumble with custard sauce was my favorite. It was simply yummy!

My first food and nutrition practical was what you would call "Hell's Kitchen". We had series of theory lessons prior to the Practical. The Topic was "Pastry making." It was not difficult to write notes on different pastries including ingredients and methods for making pastries. I had always been taught in English in Nigeria and A-level in Nigeria prepares you for university. Still, I had never came across the following:

- Flaky pastry,
- Rough puff pastry,
- Hot water pastry,

- Choux pastry,
- Short crust pastry.

The practical lessons started with short crust pastry. I had never heard the word "Short crust pastry" but I'd eaten meat pie, fish pie and chicken pie in Nigeria.

I was taught how to use the Kitchen scale to weigh ingredients for short crust pastry which is half fat to flour with a pinch of salt. Hands must be cold, using finger tips to rub the fat into the flour until the mixture looked like fine bread crumbs. You would then add cold water, a little at a time until you got a nice firm pastry.

I got it all right, until my lecturer said, "Using a rolling pin, roll with short light even strokes". I took the rolling pin, banged it on the pastry and grinded the pastry as if I was using the local grinding stone in Nigeria. My lecturer shouted and said "Christie stop! Stop!" She repeated saying "Christie, I said short light even strokes". I had no clue what she was talking about; I thought I was to grind like grinding in the Nigerian context.

I burst out crying in front of all the other students unable to control my emotions. These were things I had never done in Nigeria. I think she realised she had gone a little overboard. She sat me down in her small office next to the food room and explained step by step how to roll short crust pastry including the shaping, lifting and light strokes. I felt humiliated in the presence of all the white students.

It is well over forty-three years now and I can boast that I still make the best short crust pastry. The colder your pastry the better. With a perfect pastry, you do not need to dredge your board or rolling pin. The outcome is just a perfect short crust pastry!

Six weeks had gone so quickly. It was half term. It was impossible for me to travel to Nigeria for One week. My aunty in London had travelled to Nigeria as well. I knew I had no choice than to stay in my hall of residence.

Surprisingly, my school Mentor Linda invited me to come with her to Newcastle Upon Tyne for half term, which was for a week.

Newcastle Upon Tyne! I was more than convinced

that that place would be worse than Liverpool and I was not ready for questions and funny looks. She managed to convince me that a change of environment would surely help me mentally and psychologically.

Would it?

We took a train to Newcastle Upon Tyne from Liverpool station. On our journey, I got dirty looks from passengers as usual but I had now grown accustomed to it. Already I could predict what would happen during the next six days at Newcastle. Her parents were at the station to pick us up. They were warm and very friendly and received me with open arms. Amiable couple indeed, very congenial. On arrival at their house, her siblings gave me a hug one after the other which felt quite strange considering what I had gone through in Liverpool. This was something I did not expect. They were a genuine family. Dinner was served, so much to eat, drink and talk about. For the first time in six weeks, I felt at home with this beautiful, accommodating, genuine and generous family. Nothing was hypocritical or duplicitous about them.

As expected, the following morning, some neighbors came to say hello to me. I could feel the curiosity. Questions were asked like "Where do you come from?" "Are you going back to your country after your studies at the university?"

Whether the questions were genuine or not, that is left for posterity to judge.

I really enjoyed my stay at Newcastle Upon Tyne. Till I left school, I was forever grateful to Linda and her entire family. Lectures resumed after half term and I was very much relaxed and happier now. Melanie also noticed that I was a much happier person and this made her happy as well. She tried her best to make me happy within the school.

My dad made sure he called to inquire after my welfare and progress in school. He did not fail to remind me at the end of every call that I needed to come out in flying colours no matter the circumstances.

My first year in university was a big struggle but I scaled through with the help of Almighty God and a high sense of determination, coupled with hard work. I'd watch as many students went clubbing on Friday nights to have fun while I stayed indoors to read and complete my assignments and projects. Melanie still maintained her friendship with me for the three years I was at Fl Calder. She remained what you would call my backbone; a friend in need who was a friend indeed. Melanie was a friend one would describe as not only a buddy but a confidant and bestie. There was so much work to cover! How other students managed to get their work done was something that puzzled me. I had to read triple hard to succeed. It was at the end of my first year that I decided I had a story to tell in future based on my experience so far.

CHAPTER THREE

A year had gone so quickly. How time flies! On resumption in the second year, I sighted a black woman in college. I was over the moon. Her name was Anna Sowley from Ghana. Someone from Africa WOW! My joy new no bounds; I was no more the only coloured girl. I quickly ran into her arms, introduced myself and gave her a tight hug. She told me she was from Ghana and I told her I was from Nigeria. She replied by saying Ghana and Nigeria are sisters and neighbours. Being a matured woman, she could not stay in the hall of residence. She told me she had gotten accommodation in town close to Granby Street, inner Liverpool. I was a bit upset that she would be staying in town. She noticed that my countenance changed and she reassured me that we would have fun together and that I could visit her any time.

Anna Sowley was a very fun-loving woman. She was full of life, understanding and accommodating. She'd come from Ghana to achieve her Certificate in Education, which is a year's course. Every Saturday morning after cleaning my room and spending 3 hours doing my homework, I would pay Anna a visit in town. She was always welcoming. She taught me how to prepare different Ghanaian dishes. Banku and grilled fish, Waakye, Kelewele, Kokonte, Palm nut soup, Kontomire and Plakali. I was very keen to learn how to cook all these dishes being a food nutrition student. She would explain all the different ingredients to me one by one. After a good meal, we would sit down and exchange ideas about Nigeria and Ghana. We talked about sensitive issues on racism based on her experience and how I was able to live with racism in Liverpool. Anna made me understand that if I make racism an issue, it would affect my studies and I would lose focus. She explained to me that experiencing racism was a "storm" that was testing my faith, but that racism could not steal what is inside of me. She told me that racism can only "bark" or "bite" but hasn't got what it takes to consume us. She always reminded me to stop overrating racism anytime I am faced with it that the power of God in us cannot be depleted by any form of racism that comes our way. That was how I developed that earth shaking faith and determination to excel. She pleaded with me to navigate the three years in university very well and not be distracted in any way.

I also realized that if I continued to make racism an issue, it would only continue to wreak havoc in my life. It was imperative for me to make sure my attitude was in line with God's word so as to have strong faith and in the end become victorious. I was now focused on how good God was to me. I became an overcomer and He delivered me from all forms of racism that had put my soul and body in bondage since I had arrived in Liverpool.

I got rid of all my fears and doubts and looked expectantly at what I knew God was able to do in my life. My constant prayer now was "I shall not be weary and that my spirit will not faint." I shook off every fear, every racist comment and declared by faith that "It is well with me." Therefore, I told myself constantly that no racism as a black girl would affect me. And my prayer was that every racist comment to destroy my life would be frustrated in Jesus name.

There were times Anna and I would go shopping at Granby Street to buy African foodstuffs. The market was close to the sea port and on investigation I was told that many blacks who were sailors retired and also settled at Granby Street. There was also a prominent club which was called "Yoruba Club." It was always packed full on Fridays and Saturdays with Nigerians who were mostly Yorubas but they welcomed other Africans as well. Houses at Granby were dilapidated and very old.

Anna had a lot to tell me about Ghana; their way of life, education system, politics and general lifestyle of Ghanaians. I would sit next to her while she told me these stories. I found a mother in Anna, any time I called her "Aunty Anna", she would say "Yes my dear" with a warm smile. She had different costumes from Ghana, very colorful ones. Sometimes, she would wear her costumes on

Saturdays when we went shopping and people would stop us and ask her where she was from. She taught me a lot about her culture, marriage ceremonies in Ghana, burials, naming ceremonies, housewarming and so on. Nigeria and Ghana were indeed sisters but our cultures were totally different. Six months of friendship with Anna Sowley, I had learnt so much about Ghana. The age difference between Anna and myself helped a lot. She exhibited so much understanding in dealing with me. She was mature and full of life with so much experience to share. Anna was a "God sent" mother figure.

A year had gone so quickly, Anna was done and dusted ready to go back to Ghana. Frustration, anxiety and fear crept in. How would I cope without Anna? I had completed my second year and was now heading into my final year. My friend and companion was leaving so soon. She sat me down few days to her departure and gave me some advice. She told me that being a "black" woman meant I would need to work triple hard. She assured me that on completion of my first degree, I would become a great woman as a result of all the challenges I had faced. Anna reassured me that my end would be better than my beginning. She said that being the only black girl in college had given me strength and I'd be able to stand in front of Kings and Queens later in life.

With heavy hearts, we finally parted. I was flooding in tears. She left for London and then to Ghana. After Anna left, I became a very strong woman. I was so determined to work very hard and come out with outstanding result. Anna had given me the strength to forge ahead and I could not afford to let her down. Meeting Anna was not a coincidence. I believe we crossed each other's paths so I could be successful in life. After she left for Ghana, we both kept in touch for four years and then lost contact.

Letters from Anna were always full of encouraging words. Words like "stay focused", "be determined", "don't be distracted", "discard all negative comments", "don't let anyone put you down.", "Use your inner strength to achieve your goals", "black people are tough and rugged…"

In one of her letters, she affirmed the fact that racism and nepotism were real but I needed to look at the top of the staircase and not below the staircase.

Looking down wouldn't permit me to get to the top and I needed to get to the top no matter my colour background or where I came from. She emphasised that I must be a survivor despite all odds. All her advice to me served as guiding factors for me to be successful. It helped me to know that she had not forgotten me.

The summer before resuming for my final year, I got a call from dad informing me that my mum would be visiting me in Liverpool. It worried me a bit that my mum was coming all the way from Nigeria to Liverpool. Dad wanted mum to meet with Mr. Kenworthy just to inquire about my performance. That was very typical of my dad! Mum arrived mid-August and was fortunate to meet Mr. Kenworthy before he travelled out to Australia for his summer holidays.

I honestly don't know what ensued or the conversation between mum and Mr. Kenworthy but when mum came out of his office, she was all smiles. All she said to me was well done! Yes, well done indeed. She didn't have the slightest idea what I had been through! Anyway, it was good to know that my mum would be delivering good news to my dad on her return back to Nigeria.

CHAPTER FOUR

I resumed for my final year in September with so much vigour. Nothing mattered to me now. Getting my degree to take back to my parents was my ultimate goal and that must be achieved especially now that my parents expected nothing less. I dared not return to Nigeria a failure. There was so much to do in my final year. With determination and hard work, I eventually made it. I had no spare time; it was unending work with constant late nights, endless cups of coffee at intervals and chocolates to go with it. I also loved my chocolate biscuits.

Coursework, thesis and teaching practice was cumbersome. I worked double hard with my lesson notes and of course, visual aids. That was something else. I would sit on the carpet cutting and pasting pictures on cardboards, using felt pens, crayons, coloured paints and all the others, you just name it! All was in a bid to get the best posters to captivate the children I would teach during teaching practice. There were also times I had to write lesson notes over and over again but I took it well without complaining as I believed my lecturers wanted me to come out best.

I was posted to a small school outside Liverpool for my teaching practice to teach food and nutrition. As usual, my first day in school for my teaching practice was a harrowing experience. The first thing I did on getting to school was to ask for the toilet. I got inside, locked the door and said to myself "Christiana, you can and you will." Never stop trying Christiana, never stop believing and never give up", I repeated to myself. I said one or two prayers, headed for the reception and asked for my class.

As I started teaching a topic on nutrients, I remember vividly, a girl raised her hands and asked "Miss, I hear you live on trees"? Another shouted "Have you got a lot of monkeys where you come from? The third pupil asked "Have people got tails in your country?"

A big test! My emotions were rattled. I said

"No, we don't live on trees. We live in beautiful houses like you. And yes, we have monkeys but they are in the Zoo." The two boys re-echoed the word "Zoo." I reassured the pupils that we don't have tails and I definitely didn't have one. I told them that I am like each and every one of them and the only difference was the colour. I moved on to ask if there was any other question before I began teaching.

"No!" The three boys shouted. Lesson on nutrients then started. Lesson continued till the bell rang. The teacher who observed me said the lesson went extremely well with clear objectives achieved. She also said I communicated with the pupils effectively throughout the lesson, with differentiation including assessment strategies. She suggested I give individual feedback to pupils in form of targets.

After a hectic day, I tried leaving school early to catch the first bus so as to get back to college on time and also to avoid getting on the same bus with some of the pupils and their parents. Once I got inside my room, I sat down on my chair sweating profusely and asking myself different questions. Did it go well? Did I handle the questions well? Was there anything else I should have said?

The following day, I met the class teacher who observed me the previous day along the corridor. She said, "Well done Christiana! You handled your class very well yesterday." I wasn't sure if her well done was genuine or disingenuous. The 6 weeks teaching practice went very well and I came out with a distinction. Now I was more determined to work harder to achieve my goal. How time flies! Three years was about to come to an end.

After my teaching practice, it was half term. The unimaginable happened. I came to London to spend my half term with my aunty. I was taking a shower when I detected a lump on my right breast. I said to myself *it can't be "C."* I phoned the surgery to book an appointment. The doctor confirmed my worst fear. After a visit to the doctor and an x-ray at the hospital, I was told I had a lump. I was referred to King's college hospital where I had more tests done and after thorough examinations, the doctor confirmed that I would need to have an operation.

Before the operation, the doctor said if it was benign, he wouldn't have to remove my breast. If not, the breast would be removed. Benign refers to a condition, tumor, or growth that is not cancerous. This means it does not spread to other parts of the body. Sometimes, a condition is called benign to suggest it is not serious or dangerous. During this traumatic period, I stayed positive because I knew I was not alone. God was by my side and he would perfect all things concerning me. As usual, I derived strength from the Almighty who had always seen me through my trials and tribulations. I held on tight, praying his will be done in my life. I kept praying while in the hospital. I did not stop praying as I waited the fulfillment of Gods glory in my life. The answer was round the corner. I told God I desire him more than anything on earth. And that even if my health fails, God remained the strength of my heart. After the operation, I gained consciousness and the first thing I did was to feel my right breast. It was there, though sore. I breathed a sigh of relief. I was discharged five days later and after another week, I returned to school, having jumped another hurdle.

Back at school, I continued to keep hope alive. Keeping hope alive was imperative to eliminate any negativity from my mind. Breakthrough was surely in sight.

My spiritual life improved as I had no one to talk to. I started to be sensitive in the spirit just to know how to go about the actualization of my vision. God became my confidant. My key prayer was that God would give me the grace to always see him in all my frustrating moments and not be tempted to despair or be discouraged before and during my final examinations.

My thesis was on Palm oil. With a lot of support from my parents and lecturers, I was able to complete it with a good grade. Final exams came with endless nights of reading and as usual, nonstop coffee. Sometimes the spirit of fear would creep in with questions like *will I end well?* As a student in Great Britain, you cannot predict what your grades would be as no one would let the cat out of the bag. After exams, you come across lecturers along the corridor, they'd give you a smile and you would wonder whether you have failed or passed your exams or perhaps have to resit some papers. Your heart starts beating heavily at the mere sight of your lecturers.

Eventually, results were released and behold I made it! A huge weight off my shoulders. I breathed a sigh of relief. The pain, agony, anxiety and frustration was over at last. I came from Nigeria three years ago with nothing. Now I'd be returning to Nigeria with something.

My hard work and high sense of determination had paid off. Despite all odds, I finally scaled through. My parents had to hear the good news; that I made it at last! I called them and informed them about my result. Mum was over the moon but dad did not show any excitement because he did not expect anything less.

Dad and mum raised us to always show gratitude to people. It was indeed tough but I owe my gratitude to all my lecturers and Mr. Kenworthy. They all supported me throughout the three years. Thus, I made sure I went to all my lecturers one by one to say thank you. On arrival in Nigeria, I also wrote a letter to Mr. Kenworthy appreciating all his love and support for the three years I spent at FL Calder.

Before heading home finally, I decided to work for six weeks. My spirit was very high; I wanted to buy small gifts for my family and friends in Nigeria. It was not easy getting a job. As usual, color was an issue. After sending applications out, I instantly got letters of interview. At the venue for the interview however, once they sighted me, "THE BLACK LADY" the next thing would be "Oh I'm sorry the job's just gone." How come I keep getting the same reply everywhere I applied for a job? It was easy to invite me for interviews because my name was Christiana Shaw. They always thought I was a white lady. Shaw was my maiden name, and it is an English name. What a shame! Eventually, I got a job after so many applications. The last job offered to me was one I had to fight for. Just as the manager saw me, I said to him "Please don't tell me the job's just gone because I'm a black lady". He replied "Oh no! The job's available; all I need to do is take your details and ask you a few questions." That was how I finally got the job. What an experience! I had to fight my way through and I was able to reach my potentials with the application of self-discipline.

After six weeks, I was ready to go back to Nigeria, serve my country and work for Western region. They had awarded me the scholarship after all. It was good to be home; a big relief in the midst of my family and friends. There was so much to talk about and experiences to share. During the first two weeks, I was treated like a queen amongst my family members. There was so much to eat and drink, cousins and old friends came visiting as well. I had the opportunity to share photos and to give them gifts, sweets and chocolates which I bought from the UK.

CHAPTER FIVE

By the third week, I had to register for my NYSC programme; Nigerian Youth Service. Every Nigerian graduate is expected to take part in this programme. The National Youth Service Corps is a programme set up by the Nigerian government to involve Nigerian graduates in nation building and the development of the country. This is also known as national service year. I had my orientation at Oshodi, Nigerian army rehabilitation Centre in Lagos. It was an interesting experience meeting graduates from different universities and Nigerians who also studied abroad. Some of us who had come from abroad struggled to take part in the difficult exercises but it was fun. After the orientation, I was posted to Ifako Teachers Training College, Agege Lagos for the remaining months of my youth service. I was fortunate again to work with Mr. Adeniyi; a man we called Papa Adeniyi. He was a seasoned educationist with vast experience. The vice principal was Mrs. Ajayi. Here I had to teach adults, some as old as my mother. My head of department was Mrs Abidekun, she too studied Home Economics in UK. We got on very well and later got to know that she was related to my fiancé. Irony of life. Mrs Abidekun became so involved with all my wedding preparations. Her involvement was part of the success of the wedding ceremony.

On completion of my NYSC, I decided to get married to my boyfriend after 9 years of courtship. It was a big wedding in Lagos and both parents were very happy that it happened at last. I was married to someone who was not only my boyfriend but my best friend, confidant and soul mate. We were so fond of each other and nothing has changed after forty-two years of marriage

I got a job at Command Secondary School Ipaja (CSSL), a school for not only uniformed men and women but also for civilians.

While at command, I had my three children.

The first was a girl followed by two boys. The first and second delivery went well. The third was rather challenging but I survived it. One interesting thing my husband and I did was that after the birth of each child, we'd take the new baby to a Catholic Cathedral church close to the hospital and put the child in front of the altar before heading home. The three children were born at St Nicholas hospital. God as usual was always first in my deliveries. St Nicholas hospital was owned by Dr Olikoye Majekodunmi, the first Sole Administrator of old western region during the crisis between Action group and Nigerian National Alliance party. The hospital was known for its high standard and things were really easy for me because my husband's cousin, Dr. Victor Muyiwa Taiwo was working there. He gave me confidence that I wouldn't have problems with my deliveries. He was a strong believer in family ties and would do anything to put his extended family first. His wife was always supportive during my child bearing days. Expensive hospital but you get the best medical facilities and nurses very caring.

At Command Secondary School, I taught

Food and Nutrition at the senior level for approximately 18 years before retiring. When I began teaching at Command, Mr. Ajayi was the Principal (civilian). After him, we had military principals called Commandants; the likes of late Col Lawal, late Col Obidipe, Col Ukut and Col Ekpo. I enjoyed teaching at CSSL and made food and nutrition interesting and exciting. I was able to teach them all the skills I learnt in the UK. Instead of teaching local dishes, I opted for different British dishes and recipes which they showed off during their WAEC practical examination. All the students I taught at CSSL achieved A grades throughout in Food and Nutrition. WAEC food and nutrition examiners were always impressed with the students' creativity, presentation skills, garnishing of dishes and laying of tables to the highest standard.

Students were taught how to choose different dishes, order for dishes of their choice, costing, preparation, cooking, and most importantly, cleaning and clearing up. They found me to be a very strict teacher but also one who had real passion for food and nutrition. I taught them food and nutrition beyond school and into a wider world. My lessons were seasoned with posh English and sometimes, they struggled to understand me-same thing that happened to me when I was a student in Liverpool. All I was trying to do was to "captivate" their interest in my subject. I remember teaching Gumsu Abacha and her best result was in Food and nutrition. I remember teaching one of my husband's cousins Miss Tolu Bankole now Mrs Oshodi. Every time I visited her dad at Ipaja, the first thing he would say is "Tolu has just cooked me a sumptuous meal, thank you for teaching her how to cook at Command." One of my colleagues at CSSL, Miss Joy Elumelu now Mrs. Joy Odita, contributed immensely to my success at Command Secondary. She was an inspiration to me throughout my journey at the school. She had such a high sense of humor and there were no dull moments when she was around. Sometimes, work was overwhelming in the Home Economics department especially when we had Brigadier's and Colonels visiting the school from the army education headquarters. Looking through the windows, once we sight green vehicle coming with flags in front heading for the Commandants office, we start running helter skelter putting finishing touches to all the dishes prepared. We always had to cook a variety of dishes with impressive setting, colorful, mesmerizing and tantalizing foods. The set up was always captivating and mouthwatering as you walked into the Home Economics room. In the heat of the moment when preparation was at the highest peak with everyone running and sweating, changing different chopping boards for different food items, Joy would crack a joke and members of the team would start laughing creating a light mood. Red chopping board was for meat, green for fruits, brown for vegetables, blue for fish and white was for bread or dairy products. She made challenging work so easy with her attitude as well. She was also a very creative individual and a combination of the two of us in Home Economics helped to create an outstanding image for the department. She was an excellent team player, always ready to support me as the head of department and very loyal to the end. Joy popularly called "joy girl" eventually became a personal friend and confidant. Our relationship grew beyond school and later, she relocated to the UK where she went into Nursing and now a Matron.

After retiring, I was opportune to meet some of my old food and nutrition students either at the airport or at special occasions. It gives me great joy because they take me back down memory lane, reminding me of some of the things I used to teach them in class. *Short crust pastry, half fat to flour. Use your finger tips to rub the fat into the flour, short light even strokes when rolling short crust pastry. Creaming butter and sugar; the more you cream the better your cake, the better your cake the more you cream, cream cream cream and cream.* Cooking was fun at Command Secondary School and there were times I would come up with a song to make the lesson enjoyable

There were also times the lesson would come to an end with me shouting none stop. Especially when it came to cleaning and clearing, storing food items back in the fridge, freezers and cupboards.

Some still remember how I taught them how to cook spaghetti bolognese and till date, they cook it for their families. I have also had the opportunity to meet some of their husbands and the way I'm introduced gives me goose flesh at all times, lifts my spirit and makes me fulfilled as a teacher.

I retired from Command secondary school as Head of Department.

On retiring, I decided to relocate back to the UK with my children to give them the best education just as I had received. I made them understand that it would be tough with so many obstacles but I gave them the assurance that we would sail through. I was not afraid to start again. This time, I was not starting from scratch but starting based on "experience". Before I left, I had a Secondary and Primary school called Catlad group of schools. It took off well with sixty-five students resuming on the first day. I was really encouraged with the number. Having the school did not discourage me from taking my children to the UK. I left someone in charge of the school with 6 teachers for the initial take off. On arrival in London, we managed to get a one room apartment in Dalston. The room had one double bed and a double mattress that we put on the floor every night. I was able to get the children into a school close by. They still had to take the bus every day however. I got an early and late cleaning job to keep and feed the children including paying the rent. Britain had changed compared to when I came to study. More black people were everywhere on the streets of London. I made the children understand that things were way better than my schooling days. They enjoyed school and integrated very well into the society which I did not have the opportunity to enjoy when I came to study. After the first month, I was really struggling with feeding the children, so I took on another job in a bread factory in Finsbury Park to sustain the family. The three jobs provided for our basic needs at least for the initial period. The children would have a cup of tea, one slice of bread and then they were off to school. This continued to the end of year.

Christmas was like every other day. There was nothing to celebrate as we could not enjoy that joy of Christmas. Why? We could not afford it! We had a black and white Television that kept us company anytime we were all together in the room. Before turning on the Television, we would have to bang it twice for it to work properly. Shopping was done once a month and we shopped at the cheapest supermarket. When shopping, we would compare prices and go for the cheapest chicken, milk, butter, washing up liquid, bathing soap, bread, vegetables and fruits with expiry dates in two days' time. December in the room was so cold. The heater was not working so each one of us had a hot water bottle that we wrapped in towel and always held to our chests. Once it was cold, we would boil water and change the hot water. After one year, I got a full-time job with a catering industry and would work from six am to six pm. On the way home, I would sleep on the bus, and drag my feet after getting off, until I knocked on the front door. The children were very helpful during this period. Before getting home, they would have prepared the meal for us to eat. The more I worked the more tax I paid. Life was tough but bearable, much better than when I came as a student.

After 4 months, I was sent by my agency to work with Sodexho; a catering company with Salvation Army at Whitechapel "Boot House" which was a place for the homeless. When going home, the manager would ask us if we wanted nearly expired foods from Sainsbury or Tesco. I would gladly take stuff because it helped to feed my family. Every time he asked us to take the expired foods, I was always over the moon. Sometimes this is what we would eat for a week or two due to financial constraints. I had to pay all my bills because the money I was earning was not enough to cater for all my needs.

My children's demands increased more and more, So I decided to opt for another job very close to Boot house. During my one-hour break at Boot House, I would take my uniform off and run to do the second job next door. The building was an extension of Salvation Army. I would rush in, sweep, clean, mop, and pick used syringes.

One day, a friend of mine with whom I worked in the kitchen, Funmi Olubiyi offered to help me with my one-hour cleaning job because I was running late. When she saw the job I was doing, she nearly cried. After I finished my work, she called me to a corner and in a nice firm way, told me that I should not go back to the job again because it was not good for my health and if anything happened to me, I would regret. I took her advice and stopped the work at once. I could identify the health risk initially but because I needed money to sustain my family, I kept going. Funmi Olubiyi was another Joy Odita. Very hard working, consistent, reliable and dependable. Not for one day was she absent from work. She would arrive half an hour before we start cooking and will not leave until everything was set for the following day. She was a well cultured and respectable lady. Now in full catering. Not surprised because she always had what it takes to be successful in life.

We had serious issues with accommodation and there were times we were constantly moving from one accommodation to another. From damp areas to accrued bills, gas not working and blocked sink or toilets, most of the accommodations we lived in were not conducive for animals not to talk of human beings. Some did not have hot water and we had to boil water to have our bath. Eventually, we decided to upgrade ourselves from one bedroom to a one-bedroom flat also in Dalston. Barely a month after we moved into the one-bedroom flat, I came back from work only to find that the house had been boarded. The landlord owed the council a year's rent. There was nowhere to go. We all had to sleep on the staircase till the following morning. This was an act of overcoming challenges in order to achieve my goals. It was freezing but we derived warmth from each other. This was a harrowing experience, very painful and traumatic.

Due to the problems we had with the landlord, we had to move into a friend's house in Mile End. Shortly after moving in, on a Sunday afternoon, I was jolted out of my thoughts by a knock on the door. On opening the door, I saw two hefty men in immigration uniform. They flashed their ID card and asked politely if they could come in. They were looking for the landlord. Unfortunately, they did not ask after our identity, but I told them we were there temporarily. By the look of things, the Landlord had immigration problem.

Immediately they left, we started packing our stuff for fear that they might come back again and if they did, we might not be that lucky. We spent the following day looking for another accommodation. Fortunately, we got a one-bedroom flat at Shernall Street in Walthamstow. The garden was filthy and the kitchen looked like a box room but we wanted peace of mind. We got this accommodation from an agent.

In total, we had moved into 10 different apartments within four years. I had to take on an additional caring job in a home in Epping on Saturdays and Sundays just to meet up with the rent.

In between, my husband would visit from Nigeria and encourage us from time to time. We cultivated the habit of praying and fasting at all times. This made us a strong and united family. Prayer, faith and hope was the "Key." When we were in Walthamstow, my husband came visiting and he was able to identify the fact that we were struggling seriously. He then decided to stay back to support me. The timing was just right.

When my children were in secondary school, I would take the bus to work and back. I noticed that there were always issues with black kids getting into trouble with the police. In the evenings, as I returned from work; I would see gangs of six or more black boys smoking, threatening passersby, or vandalizing windows of shops. What I saw on daily basis gave me constant fear, especially as a black mother with "three black kids". Would I be able to keep my children safe, out of trouble and focused without peer influence?

Every night I returned from work, this fear would creep in. Would I cope without my children being victims in an exposed society where children always had their way?

My inner thought was that no matter what, my own children would be successful. Where I come from, our cultural belief is that when children are taken abroad to study, they have to come out in flying colours and bring glory to the family name not shame. I was full of hope, dreams and ambition for my children. Tough as it may seem, I'd been there before and I didn't want them to end up at the "The Juvenile detention" or "Young Offenders Home". Neither did I want their names tarnished for future job opportunities in the UK.

As a family, we had our set rules. Once back from school, it was lunch, homework, projects and then dinner at 7pm.Television was next; East enders, Emmerdale Coronation Street and family affairs, switching from one station to the other until 9pm and then it was straight to bed in preparation for another school day. Weekends were spent cleaning, washing and shopping for basic needs. Daily and weekly routine was very consistent. I monitored my children like a plague. I refuse to allow them socialize apart from few friends at school. I was grateful that they understood all my genuine concerns and intensions for them to succeed in life despite all odds.

After dinner on Sundays, we would sit together and discuss key issues. Things that happened in school during the week, things that went well and what needs to be done better. I would finish off by recounting my expectations of them and how the family must not fail. We had to be successful not only as a "family" but as a "black family." I made them understand that it was a great privilege for them to have the opportunity to study in the UK. Never did I forget to compare education as it was at the time to when I came in the seventies. Now, blacks had better opportunities once they were focused and willing to learn.

I could see the looks on their faces. Without saying a word, I knew that all would end well and I was reassured that they would not let me down. Eventually, they made it despite all odds. We fought to survive and we made it. My weekly advice was that we must not face family humiliation when we eventually returned to Nigeria. When it rains, it pours but soon the sun shines again. Is there anything one loves in life than for their children to do well? The sun must shine again

In between I must say we met with uncommon, unmerited and unusual favour. When the favour of God steps in, it swallows all rules and regulations. Favour covers mistakes at all times and the works of our hands are established by the Almighty God. Whoever you are and whatever you do, do your best as my three children did their best at all times. God broke protocols for their sake.

CHAPTER SIX

Guilt really worked when my children were in school because they saw how hard I worked and they wanted to make me happy. At the same time, they wanted me to be a proud black woman and mother.

The three of them went to different universities. The University of Greenwich, Middlesex University and London Metropolitan University. It was always a thing of joy to see them graduate with other students from different countries. Graduation days eased the pain in me. Every graduation was followed with a family get together, they deserved it.

On their graduation, I made sure that my husband and I looked stunning in our Nigerian traditional wear, to prove to people that we were Nigerians and our children were graduating. They had graduated without the pain I went through. How remarkable!

Shortly after they graduated, I had a major operation at Newham General Hospital. The operation was a bit traumatic for me. A total hysterectomy; it took me six months to get back on my feet. It was a real struggle. With the support of my daughter, I was able to pull through. I will forever be grateful to her, as she went all out to care for me during that period. It was a struggle to lift, bend, bath or walk long distances. My whole tummy felt empty.

There was a lot to be thankful for and gratitude was an altitude for me. I turned my focus towards all that was positive in life and I always felt better about myself and entire family.

They eventually got good jobs and married. The first two married in Nigeria and the last one in London. There was so much to show for all my hard work on them. The whole house became empty when the all left home. There was no one to scold or nag. The irony of life! A noisy home had turned virtually to a ghost house. If a pin dropped, you could hear it now. I missed them so badly, but that's life! I had the opportunity to see them at weekends but it was not the same. A new chapter in their life had begun.

With all the children leaving home, I decided to go back into full teaching which is my profession. I applied to a school in Tottenham, Parkview Academy. I got a job as a food technology teacher after CRB checks, certificate verification from University of Liverpool and references.

I would leave for work at 6am on the dot to get to work for half seven in the morning. A bus from Eastham to Stratford, from Stratford to Walthamstow and then a bus going to Woodgreen that would drop me right in front of Parkview Academy. With a heavy bag on my left arm, my special cup with hot tea and my bus pass, I dared not lose the bus pass as it was a monthly bus pass.

On getting home every night, I would rub my left shoulder repeatedly with a Nigerian balm called *Aboniki;* a very hot balm.

My ability to teach well using a collection of skills made me a highly successful teacher. Apart from being a teacher of food technology, I was also the assistant head of year 8. I was able to deal wisely with very challenging students based on my past experience. School trips were exciting and it always gave me the opportunity to appreciate students outside the classroom as they were exposed to working and playing together as a team. Team work was the key factor during school trips, quite exhausting but ended up being so meaningful. Eventually, I moved from being assistant head of year to Head of Design Technology. I always started my lesson with a review of the activity from the previous lesson, ground rules were always established and I had a range of teaching, learning and behaviour strategies. I made sure there were differences in my lessons including assessment strategies.

I exhibited my job with consistent excellence and offered creative ideas for change and improvement. As head of department, I was diligent and responsible and carried my team members along with me at all times. I was undeterred by the fact that as a team leader, one has to be extremely patient with every member of the team as they all come from different backgrounds. Fine Art was incorporated into Design and Technology. This was an area that I really struggled with. It was one of my weak areas coupled with the fact that the department was in a different building so it was a struggle checking and supporting them on daily basis. The responsibility was huge no matter how much I enjoyed my job. I realized that the distance from Eastham to Tottenham was taking its toll on me. I'd wake up tired and return tired. Traffic along Blackhorse Road did not help my situation. There was so much road works going on at the time. My body was beginning to give me signs that I needed to slow down. As a teacher, I wanted to be effective in class and to be effective, there was need to look for a nearby school. I spent 8 years at Parkview and ready to move on. I was aware that the devil you know is better than the angel you don't know, but health is wealth, hence my leaving a school where I really enjoyed teaching students from different backgrounds.

I managed to get a school; Brampton Manor Academy close to where I lived. When I attended the interview at Brampton Manor Academy, I was shocked to see that the head teacher was a Nigerian; Dayo Olukoshi. For an instant, I flashed my memory back to the seventies when I came to study.

During the interview, all he was interested in was the best candidate who would give him outstanding results.

With Dayo, it was the best or nothing. I knew I was not a lazy person so I would be able to get him the best results he wanted. The Catering department had just been renovated to a very high standard with the best industrial equipment to set the ball rolling for Hospitality and Catering, so there was no excuse for under achievement. The Catering room was like an industrial kitchen. I did my very best to keep it clean till I left the school. My hospitality students made cleaning after cooking a priority.

At Brampton, I met Mrs Titi Bello a Nigerian woman full of passion, determination and strength. She commanded so much respect from students and teachers alike. She was my type of person and the type you'd refer to as a "seasoned teacher".

During break, we would have lunch together and discuss issues relating to black kids within the school. This was something that gave both of us a lot of concern. Every time we saw black students misbehave, we would stop and counsel them, using ourselves as examples and emphasizing the need for them to stay focused, excel and graduate with outstanding results. Because Mrs. Bello and I shared this passion, we became very close indeed. Funny enough, the students always listened to us regardless that we were not their form tutors. We found time to catch up with them during break, after school and at the bus stop. We encouraged them to spend their time reading and making the best of the opportunity they were blessed with.

Sometimes, Mrs Titi would make it a personal matter; chasing them to complete their coursework and other times, staying behind to support them even when it wasn't her subject specialty. She always wanted to make a difference in the lives of students no matter where they came from. I love teachers who genuinely have a passion for their job and even go out of their way to make a difference in the lives of students. By genuine, I mean teachers who are not too faced but just get on with their jobs without looking for favour from the management. Mrs Bello had special shoes, one was black and the other brown. When she wore the black shoes, walking down the corridor, you hear this repeated tapping. “pitter-patter, pit-a pat”. When she wore her brown pointed high heels, you would hear click -clack down the corridor. Oh! her shoes made me laugh. Very smart lady wearing such expensive shoes. She wears the best.

The head teacher, Dr Olukoshi went out of his way to personify integrity at all times. He was a leader who radiated inner strength. He built his strength by not talking about it but by achieving results, along with the power of self-discipline to achieve and sustain success. He had the ability to work towards slated goals and achieved his potentials. He gave Brampton Manor a new name and a new image. OFSTED report was outstanding. He was a man who earned respect with emotional strength, vision and high momentum. He loved and enjoyed his job. He was not unaware of it, but I learnt so much from him. The things I learnt from him have helped me in the effective running and management of my school, CATLAD GROUP OF SCHOOLS LAGOS

NIGERIA.

Having experienced so many stigmas in the seventies, I realized that things had changed. The stigma was no more in existence.

The catering room was more like a typical restaurant. Quite a number of students showed keen interest in Catering. They were supportive, focused and very hardworking. My department catered for all the different events within the school, which was part of their coursework. It was very stressful but the students made my work really easy. I worked extremely hard to achieve the high standard Dr Olukoshi had set for the school and knowing him so well, I knew he would not compromise. Every time there was an event, students would wear chef hats and uniform with clog shoes, they always looked amazing! Events were always highly successful. I put in a lot of concerted effort and was able to discover their inner ability at all times. Hospitality and Catering students at Brampton Manor created outstanding careers for themselves in Catering. God almighty gave me the strength and direction to do my job as it should be done.

After three years at Brampton Manor, I knew it was time to return back to Nigeria. Leaving was not easy but I was more than determined to return home and work hard on my own school.

When I informed Dr Olukoshi that I was leaving, he wasn't too happy but I made him realize that it was time for me to invest fully into my school in Nigeria. At the end of term party for teachers leaving, he made me understand that if things didn't work out well in Nigeria, I could easily come back. But I was determined that things would work and must work no matter what I met on ground.

Going back to Nigeria was not the easiest decision to make but it was time. I did not raise my hopes and was not expecting it to be all rosy but on arrival, I met with a lot of disappointments. I remembered what Dayo told me but was not ready to go back.

CHAPTER SEVEN

Now, I believed I had achieved another goal in life. Not as a teacher in UK but as a parent of three black and successful children. It was through the grace and power of the Almighty God. He made this journey less painful than my initial journey in the seventies. I had something to show for all my hard work and determination. I had also cultivated the habit of positive thinking at all times. I used my power of vision to see the bright future that God had laid before me. This took away every hindrance towards the realization of my vision. I was able to remind myself of all the good things God had done for me and my family.

God had made my bitter water sweet. Just as Joseph in the Bible never stopped listening to the voice of God despite many years he spent in problem,

I never stopped listening to the voice of God in all my trials and tribulations. He led me to the divine purpose for which I was created.

"Success is a path", one perpetually under construction, frequently filled with detours and obstacles. I saw all my problems as mere obstacles on the path to victory.

Now the word of Isaiah came to pass *"I will keep him in perfect peace, whose mind is stayed on you"*. I believed in God who believed in me. Jeremiah also wrote *"for I know the plans I have towards you declares the lord, plans to prosper you and not to harm you, to give you a hope and a future"* My doubts did not betray my dreams. I was disciplined enough to master my problems and refuse to allow the situation to master me. "My success was born from "adversity" and Discipline kept me at the very "TOP". God was on my side and because he was on my side, I was able to cross the RED SEA, believing and trusting in God.

The first time I came to Britain to study in 1975, I did not envisage that it would be a traumatic experience because of the colour of my skin. However, when I brought my three children back to

Britain, the experience was not as bad as it was while I was studying. I knew what I wanted for them, I knew what to expect and I was full of hope, dreams and ambition. I discarded all cocktails of emotions in my brain based on my previous experience as a student in UK. I knew it would be tough as was the journey of the Israelites in the wilderness. My authentic power was with me which was my guiding factor to scale through all my hurdles. My personality served the energy of my soul as I brought the children to the United Kingdom.

Any mother should be able to give priority to her children at all times. This inner ability can never leave you as a strong woman and a mother. It is therefore of utmost importance that you perfect your inner ability in your journey of bringing up your children.

I knew that taking them to the United Kingdom was a great risk but one thing I did was that I played things by the book. I made sure that I did not collect any income support. And because of this, life was extremely tough. We had to go through a lot of pain, stress, anxiety and frustration. It was this frustration that made me seek for three jobs to keep body and soul together. I must say that my children's courage was remarkable in the midst of this wilderness; one uniform for a year, two socks and a pair of shoes, sandwiches every day, butter in between two slices of bread and half a cup of tea to school every day.

I remember how we always bought 3 bags of potatoes from Hackney Wick to serve us for a month. Fruits and vegetables were so cheap in Hackney Wick market. We had to go to the market as early as 5am in the morning to get good quality fresh fruits and vegetables. I made different dishes using potatoes like cheese potatoes, cottage pie, bangers and mash, roast potatoes with stew, chips and fish or chicken and boiled potatoes with assorted vegetables and meat stews. It wasn't difficult to create any dish as this was my profession. It was about working round your "budget." Expenditure must not be more than the income otherwise I would be in serious trouble with my finances. There was no one to turn to for a loan if I got stuck. So, I was careful to make sure I lived within my income.

We survived with prayer and hard work. God promised that he would provide for the birds of the air and lilies of the field. This was exactly what God did for us; survival without losing sanity. "Faith" was everything and at the end, it produced favourable results for the whole family despite all the pressures. My three children struggled to achieve great things and they eventually made it despite "All Odds." Their faith like mine was not dormant throughout this journey.

CHAPTER EIGHT

What I met on ground was heart breaking but I got my strength from the word of God. He said *"Is there anything impossible with me?"* Indeed not. With God, all things are possible. I was determined to turn every life situation into a positive one.

A message came directly from God that if he could see me through my wilderness journey in the UK, he would definitely fix this.

He said *"I will perfect all things concerning you."*

He promised that *"I will walk in the midst of water and I will not drown and in the midst of fire, it will not consume me because I serve a living God."*

Many places in the bible contained the short phrase "FEAR NOT", so with all these assurances I was ready to fight the battle in front of me.

Catlad group of schools had started before I decided to relocate to Britain with my children. The name "CATLAD" was coined from Christiana Ayodele Titilayo Laditan which is my full name. Initial take off with number of students was pretty encouraging. Every time I visited home, the school seemed to be making so much progress and this gave me confidence that all was well.

On returning however, what I met on ground was heartbreaking and unspeakable as my husband looked on in sympathy. Previously, Catlad schools had up to 340 students in total. When I arrived from the UK, I met only 10 students. The number I met broke my heart completely. I became confused. What would I do? The challenge in front of me was enormous but I had to face it.

God must decide for me I told myself. My hope is built on nothing else than Jesus blood and righteousness. Trust on trust on believer, though long the conflict be, though yet shall prove victorious, my God shall fight for me. My total hope and trust was in God and I was determined that the time was "RIGHT" for me to build and expand my own personal business. I'd worked very hard in different schools and now, I had to work double hard in my school.

I spent the first 2 weeks lost in thought, confusion and depression, thinking about what my next line of action should be. I was so flustered and frustrated. Eventually, after much prayer and fasting; revelation came that I had to rebuild the image of the school. I travelled to the UK with uncertainty and I pulled through all my challenges and difficult times. Why then would I not pull through my very own business?

I had to paint the school a different color so as to give it a good image, while using bright colors. I then began making one on one contact with parents who had left. I interviewed parents to know why they withdrew their children from the school, what the issues were and what they would like me to do better. On the whole, I was quick to apologize to parents and accept blame for all mistakes committed in my absence. I worked morning, afternoon and evening to make sure that parents who withdrew all their children brought them back.

Within 6 weeks of my arrival in Nigeria, I had a population of 150 students. Gradually, students and pupils increased to 240. Catlad school had bounced back with full vitality. The grace of God in action! I also acted upon advice and feedback from parents to move the school forward.

There was immediate employment of graduates who had good subject knowledge in their area of specialty. New furniture was brought in as well as improved visual aids in all classrooms. We also built Physics, Chemistry, Biology, Home Economics and Intro tech classes. Every time there was admission, I would ask the school secretary to take them round and show parents the facilities we had on ground. As a proprietress, I also taught Food and nutrition.

I introduced so many things into the curriculum based on my teaching experience in UK. Catlad School was now the talk of the town. I introduced lots of ideas to help students and pupils reach their potentials. Targets were set for individual students and students who misbehaved were put on weekly report. Parents had easy access to the school for effective mentoring. School and home worked hand in hand. News about the standard of Catlad spread like wild fire. A lot of ideas introduced at Catlad came mostly from my experience at Brampton Manor.

Having served as head of department in three different schools, I was able to build a strong team amongst the teachers. I was strict, firm, and friendly but also understanding with the teachers. At Catlad, teachers work very hard and so do students. There is commitment to collaboration and cooperative working amongst the teachers. At Catlad, teachers also know a range of approaches to assessment, including the importance of formative assessment. They also have a knowledge and understanding of a range of teaching, learning and behaviour management strategies and know how to use and adapt them, including how to personalize learning and provide opportunities for all learners to achieve their potentials.

Teachers' salaries are also paid on or before the end of each month and promoted through performance management on a yearly basis.

The school management fully understands how children and young people develop and that the progress and well-being of learners are affected by a range of developmental, social, religious, ethnic, cultural and linguistic influences.

Seminars are conducted for teachers at the start of every term. Orientation is also given to new students on admission. Effective transition takes place for primary six students going into secondary school and Form tutors are held accountable for bad behavior of students in their form. My presence in and around the school became extremely effective with easy access for parents to see me if and when needed. At Catlad, every child matters. In other words, it doesn't matter where you come from or your type of background. Anyone can come to Catlad as long as you can work hard and adhere to school rules. Students cannot resume at Catlad without presenting their Bank Tellers; evidence that they have paid their full or half school fees. Initially, parents did not like the idea but they have eventually gotten used to the system. Paying fees on resumption gives the management the opportunity to plan effectively and also pay salaries on or before the end of month. When teachers are paid on time, they are happy and teaching is effective.

CHAPTER NINE

Despite being strict and firm as the proprietress, I have an open-door policy where students can have a good chat with me on issues bothering them in and out of school. In between, we had a setback. One Monday morning, on arrival at school we realized that thieves had vandalized the school roof. They came in through the roof and ceiling in the night, stole ten laptops, eight cooking burners some equipment in the food room and cash in the office cabinet.

It was a very sad day. I felt so demoralised, cast down and daunted. After all the effort I had put in. I felt like going back to the UK in fact. What a discouragement! Sometimes life can be a bit harsh! I received so many encouraging words from family and friends and on second thought, I decided to move on and forget the whole incident. I just focused on the positives. Without this, it would have been a struggle to move forward.

Sometimes I'd sit in my office and spend time having a good look at students moving about in the school. Whenever I feel something is not right, I invite students to my office and surprisingly my instinct is never wrong. We also ensure that students wear clean uniform with black socks and black shoes which promotes the image of the school.

During morning assembly, I am always overwhelmed with joy standing in front of all the students as they sing from their songs of praise booklet, reciting the national anthem or the school anthem. Two days in a week they sing the national anthem in English, French, Yoruba and Igbo. The joy within me cannot be explained. Assembly is something students and pupils always look forward to because I always make them laugh by coming up with different stories.

Catlad is also strict with admission policy. Every student seeking admission must sit for an examination in English and Mathematics, after which an interview is conducted by the proprietress. We have a standard number of students for each class and will not exceed the stipulated number. This policy upset students but I stood my ground that I will not exceed my stipulated number otherwise the standard would fall.

We work on predicted grades for students and have a one to one with those who are under achieving. We encourage them with a program called "Push me till I pass". We push and push students till they excel in all subjects. A lot of encouragement is given to the students to ensure that they leave Catlad with so much to be grateful for in life. It is a school they will forever remember as their destiny builder.

One good thing about Catlad students is that after getting their WAEC results, they all come back to say thank you to teachers and this is what makes teachers feel fulfilled. During their visits, opportunities are given to students to discuss their future plans, choice of career and universities available in different parts of Nigeria.

Also, examinations at Catlad are conducted and supervised under strict guidance. Students who fail to achieve the specified grade to move to the next class receive counseling and are advised to retake the examinations again so as to have a good foundation for the future. At Catlad, students' welfare always comes first. Punctuality and attendance is monitored on daily basis including behavioral issues. Students are put on progress report to track improvement in behavior in and around the school. Every student is given a Diary at the start of every academic year. They write their homework in the diaries every day and at the end of the week, they assess themselves and write what they need to improve on the following week. Parents are expected to sign the diaries with dates. The Proprietress, Principal or form tutors will sign at the end of the week. This gives parents and the school opportunity to monitor performance of students from home and school as well. Parents can also visit or call the school between 8am and 3pm on daily basis to discuss issues of concern relating to their ward.

Where we have concerns with individual students based on observation, guardians, parents or carers are invited to discuss the way forward.

However, no good thing comes without its problems. One of such problems is that some parents do not agree with our policies. Some do not see reason when we raise issues with lateness to school or when students are put on red report for noise making or not completing assignments and notes in class. Some parents want teachers to be responsible for their children's behavior in school even when it comes to important values like honesty, punctuality, politeness, respect, personal hygiene, honesty and obedience to the rules. They are of the opinion that it is not part of their responsibility since school fees has been paid. One thing I always tell my students during assembly is that no matter where they go in life, the name Laditan will remain a memorabilia.

CHAPTER TEN

Catlad group of schools was built by my biological mother. She worked so hard to ensure that it was built to the required standard during our stay in the United Kingdom, putting all necessary facilities in place. We were over the moon on arrival from the UK to see how she had spent the money sent to her judiciously. In Nigeria like the rest of the world, it is sometimes difficult to trust people with your money, even your own blood. My mother however, was a woman of integrity and her accountability was second to none. I have tried to follow my mother's footsteps. Look for three things in a person. Intelligence, energy and integrity. If they don't have the last one don't bother with the first two. My mum had the last one.

She was a mother in a million. This world was so blessed to have her. She was a pillar for her family, and she did so many great things for her hometown; Akoore in Ogun state. She was involved in a lot of Community work including orchestrating complete electricity to so many villages around Ado Odo Otta Local government.

She touched so many lives in so many ways. Mum was the truest, dearest, and most compassionate woman. She was strict, she would call a spade a spade without any sentiments. She was a courageous woman who strived to do her best at all times. Speaking the truth at all times also made her a unique person.

She loved GOD with a passion, and invested a lot in the house of God. Forever, I will treasure all the values she imbibed into me.

My mum was a very independent woman. She was able to do so many things on her own even at Eighty-eight. Shortly before her 88th birthday, she became very ill and I never knew she would survive. I had to rush her to a Private hospital. Seeing her lay on her sick bed, I thought she would not make it. There were many gadgets to aid her breathing and she was unable to eat. She looked so weak and frail. With God on her side, she survived and on her 88th birthday I was able to give her a small thanksgiving celebration.

While cutting her cake, I stood in awe of her strength, energy, zeal and ability to communicate so well with individuals that attended her birthday.

She loved cooking and cooked until her last days on earth. Her grandchildren always enjoyed her cooking, especially fried meat stew with rice. She would fry the meat so dry that one can store it for weeks without putting it in the fridge or freezer.

CHAPTER ELEVEN

Forever I owe my gratitude to the almighty God, the Alpha and Omega, the beginning and the end, the Omnipotent, the One who will forever be.

After God is my best friend, soul mate, adviser, confidant, prayer partner, better half and companion. Very affectionate, supportive compassionate, dependable, above all very patient. My consort for life. That is how I would qualify my husband. When a marriage is peaceful you are able to achieve your goals in life. I was able to focus on the children because he remained faithful to the end during my absence in Nigeria.

Full of experiences of life, he could see beyond what I could not see. Based on his experience he was able to guide and support me whenever I make mistakes and lift me up when I fall. His shoulders are very strong to cry on and still strong at seventy-three. Although when he tells me off, I feel like going under the duvet to cry, but he is so quick to take me through what I did wrong and how I need to make amends. Sometimes he can be unpredictable. Not sure if this is a good thing?

God purposely bestowed the wisdom of Solomon on him. A divine gift from the Almighty.

Apart from being a teacher all my life, I have other hobbies I enjoy; one of which is match making couples. I have been successful with a total of eight couples. It's not a difficult task to match make. After setting them up, I ensure that I do a follow up from time to time.

I start off with the initial introduction, look at their academic and social background to see that they both have similarities, otherwise it might not work. It is an extremely difficult task but I derive joy in making others happy. Sometimes I find time to interview each party separately before inviting them for a meal out. The meal could also be in my house so the atmosphere is more relaxed. Match making can be time consuming, often requiring lots of patience at the initial stage. Sometimes I end up being a judge, counsellor and adviser. You must be ready to accept calls from each of them at any point in time. I never discourage even when it looks a bit rocky at the initial stage. After I have been successful and it has all ended well, I feel extremely happy that I have made others happy and been a part of their "SUCCESS STORY."

On completion of my education at Liverpool, I had this inner feeling of peace that could not be explained. The same happened when my three children were done and dusted in the UK. I was certain that I had become an overcomer. "DESPITE ALL ODDS", I tried my very best; the first time as a "STUDENT" and the second as a "MOTHER". I took the risk with my children and it paid off. As a mother, I nurtured great thoughts towards my children and the journey with them in UK was rewarding. Now, I look back with tears of immense joy not only at the thought of the goodness of God but also, the overwhelming support I got from the children as black kids in the UK. I could say that I kept them contained under my arms, and did not allow them to go astray, while trying to lead by example at all times.

This book is about bringing light to the darkness of so many Nigerians studying in the UK or who have brought their children here for a better life, and gone through pain and frustration in trying to give them the best. No doubt, so many have been successful with their children but a large percentage has got it wrong because "BLACK KIDS" are mostly overlooked.

As a black student or mother with black kids, determination is the key factor. Whatever you aim to do in life, without a strong spirit and determination you'd lose focus. Determination will help you not to be distracted. Imagine what the end product will be and develop a broader picture of the journey and definitely, you will get there. Another key factor is "PRAYER". As a Nigerian in the UK, you need to fortify yourself through consistent prayer including leading by example to your children. The children must be able to see a clearer picture of where they are heading to through you. Remind the children constantly of where they are coming from and where they are heading to. Most Nigerian mothers struggle to get a clear message in a firm but fair way to their children. And because of this, it is easy for them to go astray and end up mixing and matching with the wrong group of people. The wrong peer group can mislead you in a way that it will be difficult to retrieve your footsteps. By the time they realize the children have gone astray, it is usually too late.

This book should be an inspiration to many black mothers who leave their country for greener pastures abroad for their children. You end up with two options; to make it happen or fail to make it happen.

This book is to open a "BLIND EYE" to see beyond what no one can see "BUT YOU."

Everyone has a unique resource that can help in any situation. Everyone is different but with a determined spirit, you "CAN" and you "WILL" overcome any obstacle "DESPITE ALL ODDS."

God did not say that everything will be perfect but he did promise that he will be with us in all situations as long as we allow him to be part of our "JOURNEY". Then, he will be there for us.

Looking back at the Sixty-nine years of my existence, God has always been there for me and my entire family. I would be lying if I said that it has been easy but when I need him, I feel his presence and assurance. I hear him say *"Fear not, I will help you, do not be dismayed I am your God."*

My journey to the UK on both occasions has given me the opportunity to identify who God is, to see him more clearly and appreciate that without him; I would not have achieved anything in life.

Any journey without getting God involved can never be a successful one. He starts the journey and completes it well. Permit me to say that many mothers come into this country and forget the person who made it possible for them to get here. Getting close to God in a foreign land makes the journey much easier

In my difficult "moments", I have learnt to be "STILL" and in being "STILL", the spirit of God speaks and "DIRECTS".

COLLECTABLES

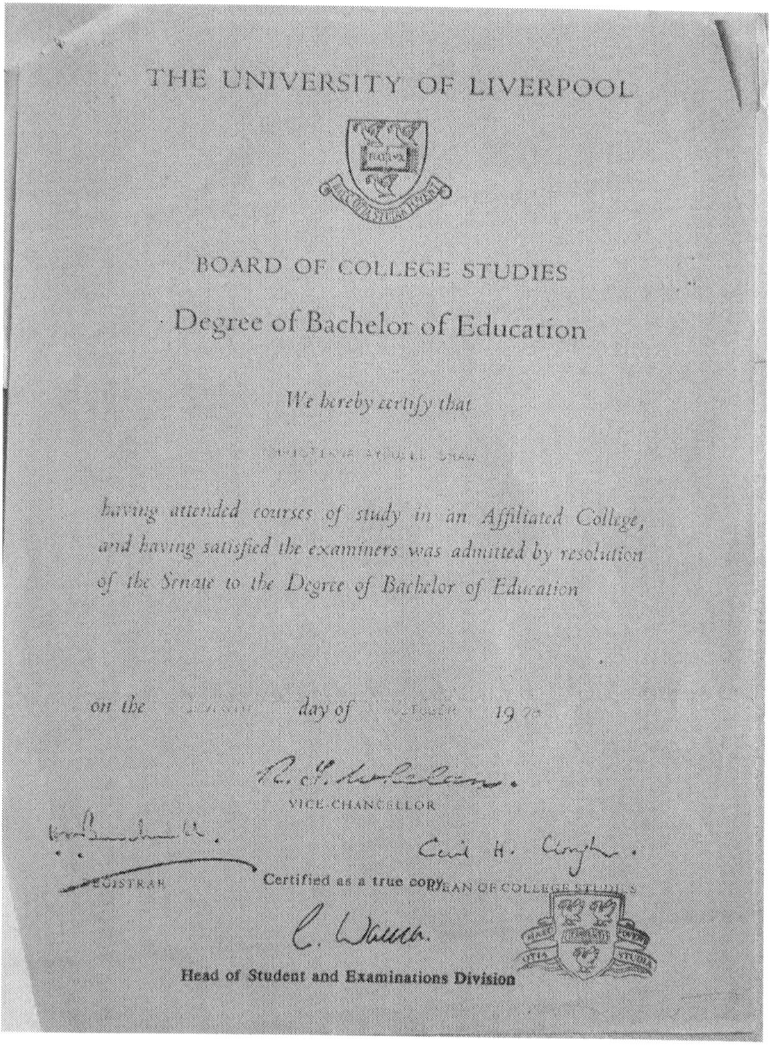
THE UNIVERSITY OF LIVERPOOL

BOARD OF COLLEGE STUDIES

Degree of Bachelor of Education

We hereby certify that

[illegible]

having attended courses of study in an Affiliated College, and having satisfied the examiners was admitted by resolution of the Senate to the Degree of Bachelor of Education

on the [illegible] *day of* [illegible] 19[illegible]

VICE-CHANCELLOR

REGISTRAR

Certified as a true copy

DEAN OF COLLEGE STUDIES

Head of Student and Examinations Division

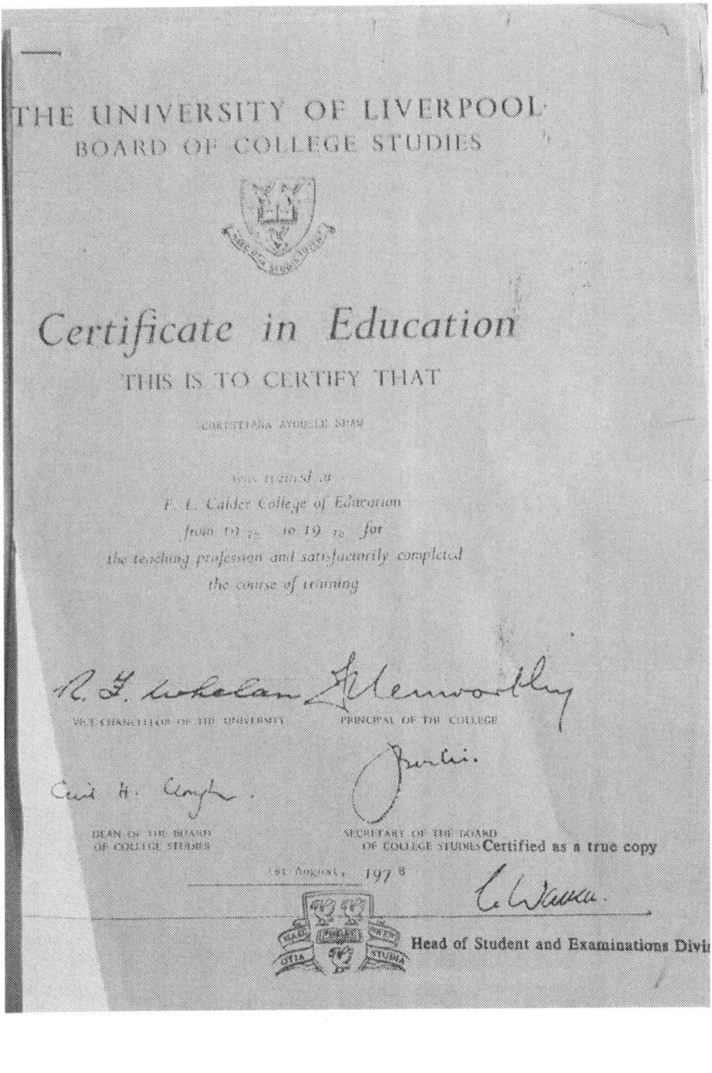

THE UNIVERSITY OF LIVERPOOL
BOARD OF COLLEGE STUDIES

Certificate in Education

THIS IS TO CERTIFY THAT

CHRISTIANA AYODELE SHAW

was trained at

F. L. Calder College of Education

from 19 75 to 19 78 for

the teaching profession and satisfactorily completed

the course of training

VICE-CHANCELLOR OF THE UNIVERSITY

PRINCIPAL OF THE COLLEGE

DEAN OF THE BOARD OF COLLEGE STUDIES

SECRETARY OF THE BOARD OF COLLEGE STUDIES

Certified as a true copy

1st August, 1978

Head of Student and Examinations Divi

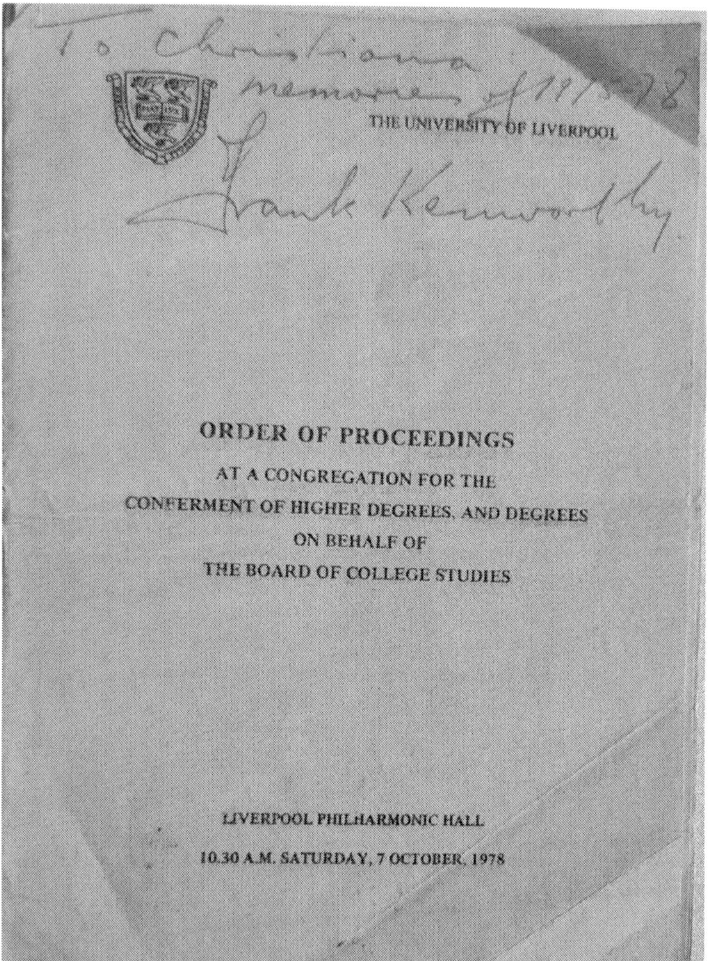

To Christiana
memories of 1975-78
Frank Kenworthy

THE UNIVERSITY OF LIVERPOOL

ORDER OF PROCEEDINGS

AT A CONGREGATION FOR THE
CONFERMENT OF HIGHER DEGREES, AND DEGREES
ON BEHALF OF
THE BOARD OF COLLEGE STUDIES

LIVERPOOL PHILHARMONIC HALL

10.30 A.M. SATURDAY, 7 OCTOBER, 1978

Ordinary Degree of B.Ed. (cont.)

* Michael Christopher Lewis
Pauline Mary Loftus
Catherine Mary Lythgoe
* Deirdre Frances McAllister
Gemma Maria McBrien
Andrea MacEachen
Veronica McGarry
Sarah Elizabeth McIlwaine
Dorothy McInerney
Mary Christine McIntyre
Gail McLean
Patricia Margaret McLoughlin
* Julie McVey
Kathryn Maguire
Kevin John William Mallinson
Janet Anne Patricia Markland
Stephen Peter Marron
Elizabeth Burden Marshall
Patricia Ann Marshall
Elizabeth Siân Matthews-Williams
Bonnie Maria Metcalfe
Carolyn Hilary Molloy
Marjorie Morris
Eileen Mary Murphy
Jacqueline Anne Neale
Anne-Marie Nicholson
Jane Susan Nicholson
Caren Teresa Nock
Colette Elizabeth O'Brien
Liam Fintan O'Brien
Jacqueline Mary O'Callaghan
Ann Marie O'Malley
Nicola Mary Palmer
Margaret Mary Parish
Susan Vickie Payne
* Lynne Pearson
Marian Pollard
Katalin Maria Eve Porganyi
Heather Power
Kathryn Powney

Ordinary Degree of B.Ed. (cont.)

Lesley Sharon Proud
Jonathan Simon Proudfoot
Anne Brigid Quigley
* Dianne Frances Ribbon
Barbara Rice
Janet Marie Richardson
Denise Rigby
Christine Lynne Robinson
Richard Andrew Robinson
Marian Rule
Patricia Ann Ryden
Rosemary Sedman
Clare Frances Shannon
* Christiana Ayodele Shaw
Joseph Patrick Shaw
Bridget Laura Skipper
Jacqueline Smith
* Helen Elizabeth Spicer
Julie Rosemary Squires
Barbara Stevens
Philip Stewart
Shelagh Ann Sullivan
Joseph Vincent Swarbrick
Marie Ann Szpak
Amanda Barbara Tarrant
* Moyra Taylor
Linda Joyce Thacker
Barbara Ann Thompson
Gillian Patricia Tomlinson
Barry Anthony Arthur Tucker
Alison Elaine Tudor
Heather Turner
Michael Anthony Ussher
Karen Elizabeth Vickers
Carole Anne Walmesley
* Elizabeth Jane Warburton
Neil Warrington
Jacqueline Webb
Frank Andrew Webster
Sylvia Margaret Webster
* Alan Whitehead

** In absentia*

9

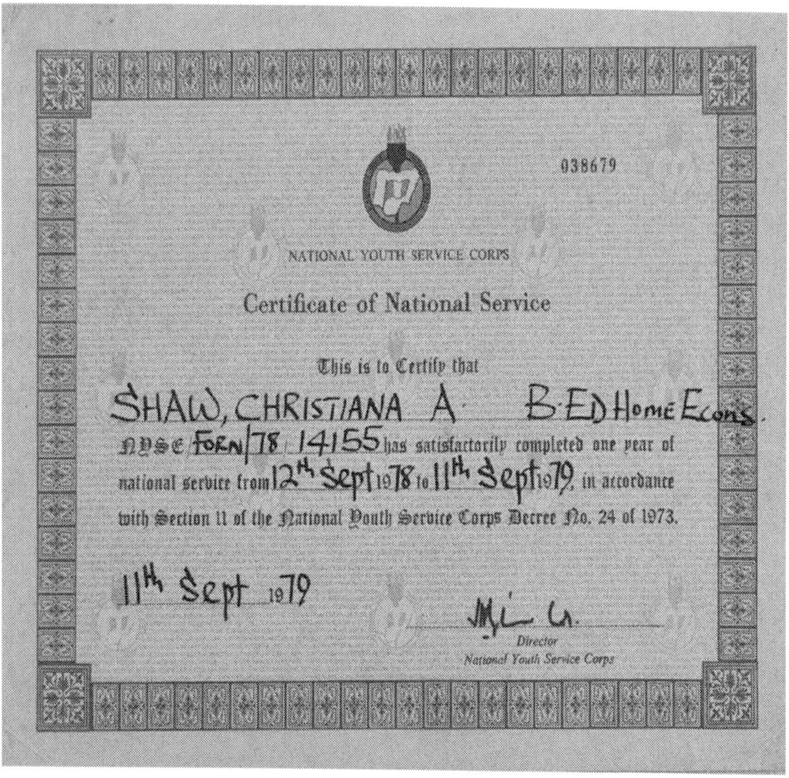

038679

NATIONAL YOUTH SERVICE CORPS

Certificate of National Service

This is to Certify that

SHAW, CHRISTIANA A. B.Ed Home Econs.

NYSC FORN/78 14155 has satisfactorily completed one year of national service from 12th Sept 1978 to 11th Sept 1979, in accordance with Section 11 of the National Youth Service Corps Decree No. 24 of 1973.

11th Sept 1979

Director
National Youth Service Corps

City of Liverpool

F. L. CALDER COLLEGE OF EDUCATION

Principal:
F. Kenworthy, B.Sc., F.R.G.S.

Dowsefield Lane,
Liverpool,
L18 3JJ.

Telephone: 051-428 4041

Miss Christiana Ayodele Shaw,
16 Okesanya Street,
Olonimsogo,
Mushin,
Lagos,
Nigeria.

11th October 1978.

Dear Christiana,

I was delighted to have your news in the letter dated 15th September, which did not reach me until 4th October. You seem full of life, as I would expect, regardless of your having to come to terms with the Nigerian climate again. I am delighted that you have been appointed to a teacher training college and I am sure that the College authorities are fortunate in having someone with your ideas, initiative and skills in service. Dont forget all the modern ideas about Home Economics! However, the thought of starting work at 8 a.m., remembering the English climate, of course, horrifies me. Its a good job that you have a mum to do her stuff. Presumably a husband will take her place in the near future!

I am sorry to hear that your father was not allowed to come to England as I had hoped to have the opportunity of meeting him. Anyway, perhaps some time in the future? Do give him my warmest regards. It is a very kind and generous thought which prompts his sending the parcel and I look forward to receiving its mysterious contents in eagar anticipation.

I attended the graduation ceremony for your year on Saturday and I thought you would like to have a copy of the programme as a souvenir. You will see that I have marked your name in red.

There are no overseas students in initial courses in the first year, though our friends Winny and Emmie continue. Howev er, the Diploma course has recruited extremely well and we have 11 students from many different countries. Several are from Africa, including two from Nigeria, two from Cameroon and one from Zambia, not forgetting another student from Malawi. Mrs. Williams from Barbados and Mrs. Lungu from Malawi did extremely well and are staying in College for a further year to study for the B.Ed. Honours degree. Unfortunately, I have been so busy with College and Polytechnic work I have only met the Diploma students for a short time and I do not really know them. But the two ladies from Nigeria, both, I believe, from Lagos, seem to have settled down.

I know that you have written to Miss Waterworth as she showed me the letter and I know other colleagues will be delighted to hear from you. We miss your cheerful, outgoing, personality and wish we had a more students like you in the pipeline. You have brought credit, not merely upon yourself, but also upon your family and your country.

Do keep in touch. If ever you return to England you know you will be a most welcome visitor here. Who knows, sometime, some of us may be enticed to Nigeria!

Every good wish to you and your family.

Yours sincerely,

Frank Kenworthy

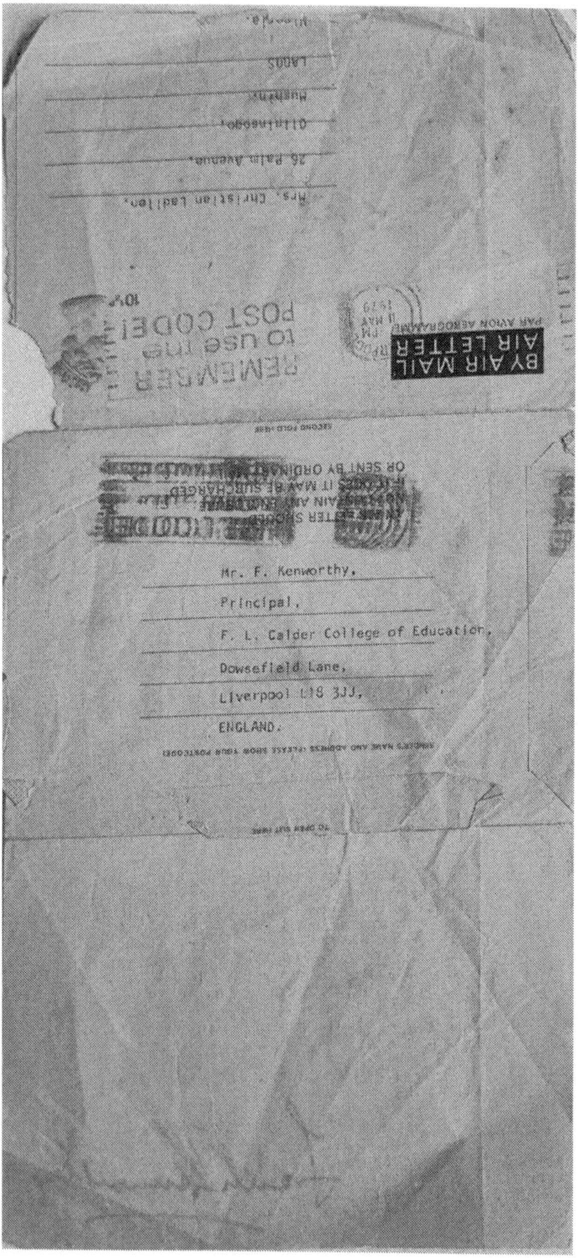
BY AIR MAIL
AIR LETTER
REMEMBER to use the POST CODE!
Mr. F. Kenworthy,
Principal,
F. L. Calder College of Education,
Dowsefield Lane,
Liverpool L18 3JJ,
ENGLAND.

LIVERPOOL POLYTECHNIC : F. L. CALDER CAMPUS

Dowsefield Lane, Liverpool L18 3JJ Tel: 051-428 4041

Mrs. Christiana Ladilen,
26 Palm Avenue,
Olinisogo,
Mushin,
Lagos,
Nigeria.

10th May 1979

Dear Christie,

How nice to be remembered especially with such a colourful picture. I am also intrigued by the flying visit to London for "an important meeting" : official or personal, I wonder. It is a pity you had not more time to dash over to Liverpool. We should have been absolutely delighted to see you again and hear of your new life first-hand. How do you find the work? I expect you will have re-adjusted to life at home once more - even the heat? At least you've been spared the most dreadfully, long cold winter of my lifetime. It is still cold despite the fact that spring should be well-advanced. Few trees are yet in leaf.

Our students from overseas have found recent months particularly hard to bear as there was a poor autumn too in 1978. Myrtle and Esther of the Diploma group last year are in the last stages of the B.Ed. (Hons.) year. Winny Suhaili and Emmie Mahlunge are thriving. We have two students from Nigeria in the present Diploma group: both most charming - as I would expect from the example set by you : a compliment in return eh! We expect one or two more next year. The Diploma course is very popular and already we are full for 1979-80. We could run two groups, but are not allowed to do so by the Government.

We have recently had an exciting few weeks leading to the election of a new parliament and government. Whether the expected changes are for the better or for the worse remain to be seen. Who knows with a woman at the helm! But I must not seem a chauvinist.

The Old Students Association has its annual reunion in College on Saturday. What about it? Your arrival would cause quite a stir, I believe. Helen Dickson has a job lined up in Isle of Wight, but I've not heard news of your other fellow students yet. Jobs do seem scarcer this year. Staff are unchanged, but Mr. Sherwen retires in July and Mrs. Atherton and Miss Young are likely to be working in the Polytechnic though legally we are still not merged with the Polytechnic even after a three year wait.

Every good wish professionally and for your married life.

Yours sincerely,

Frank Kenworthy

P.S. Thank you for the phone call. I am sorry I was not available.- next time eh!

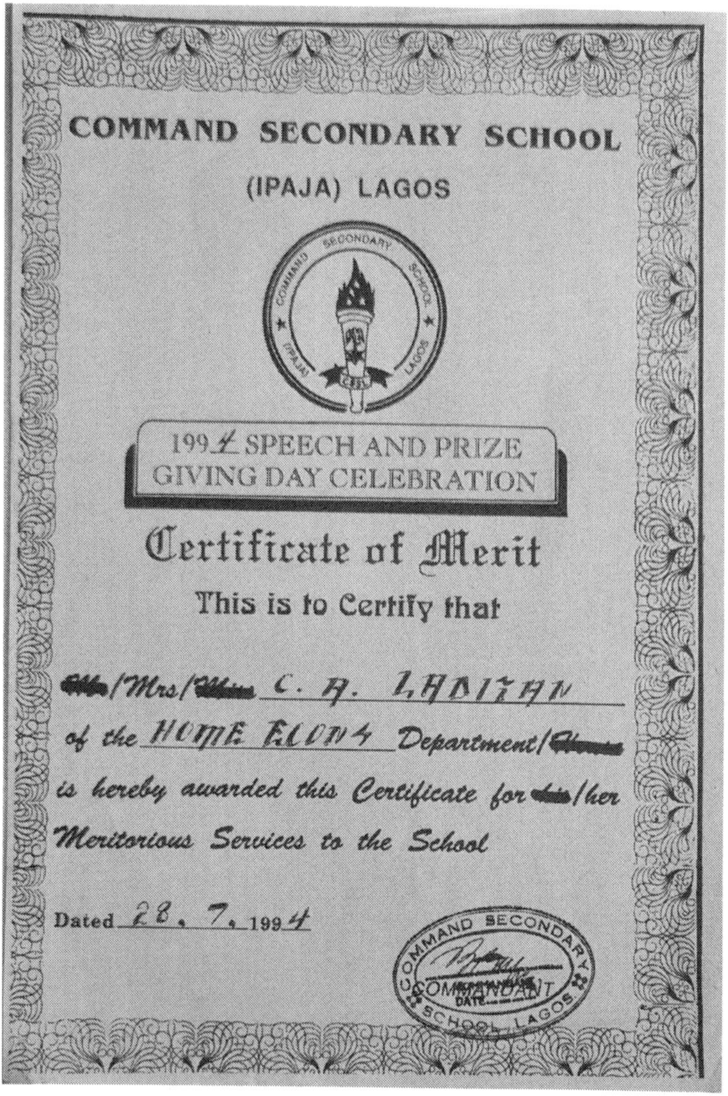

COMMAND SECONDARY SCHOOL

(IPAJA) LAGOS

COMMAND SECONDARY SCHOOL (IPAJA) LAGOS

1994 SPEECH AND PRIZE GIVING DAY CELEBRATION

Certificate of Merit

This is to Certify that

[redacted]/Mrs/[redacted] C. A. LADITAN

of the HOME ECONS Department/[redacted]

is hereby awarded this Certificate for [redacted]/her Meritorious Services to the School

Dated 28. 7. 1994

COMMAND SECONDARY SCHOOL LAGOS

COMMANDANT

DATE

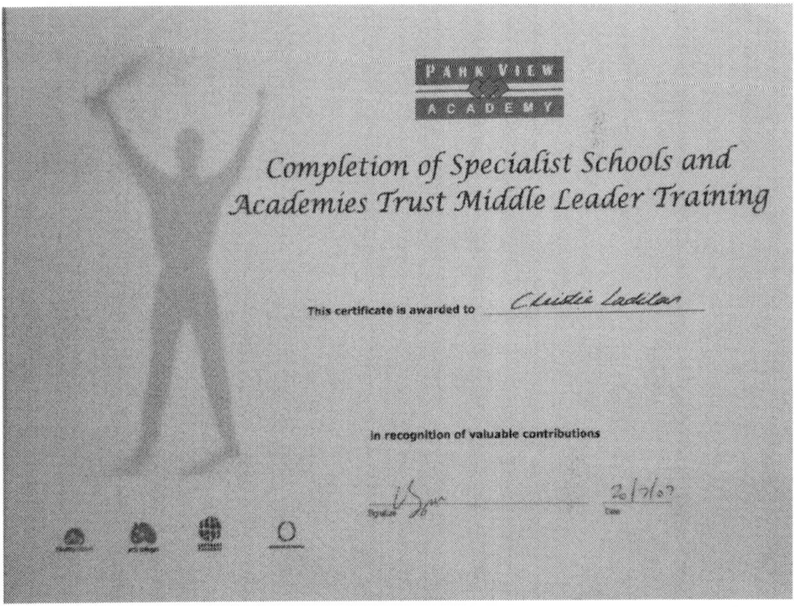
PARK VIEW ACADEMY

Completion of Specialist Schools and Academies Trust Middle Leader Training

This certificate is awarded to

in recognition of valuable contributions

Christie Laditan
Salvation Army
Greig House
20 Garford Street
London
E14 8JG

Dear Christie,

I wanted to write to formally pass on my thanks for your exceptional work at the Greig House opening on Thursday 12th July 2001. You were thoroughly deserving of all the praise and adulation that was showered upon you by those present.

You lead an efficient team – from the front – and show great loyalty and commitment to both Sodexho and the Salvation Army. It fills me with pride and confidence to know that there are people like you on my team – always willing to go that extra mile!

You have a bright future with Sodexho and many opportunities will come your way. Don't stop doing what you do so well and always remember – that you make us what we are and are appreciated for it.

Kind regards

Stephen Tomlinson
Group Manager.

Howard Cox
Regional Operations Manager.

TEN YEARS

THE TEACHING AWARDS

Nominee 2008

The Teaching Awards Trust celebrates

Mrs Christiana Laditan

Park View Academy

Lord Puttnam CBE
Chairman of the Teaching Awards Trust

Rt. Hon Baroness Williams of Crosby
Chair of the national panel of
Teaching Awards judges

BT theguardian department for children, schools and families innovation

NCSL National College for School Leadership ROYAL AIR FORCE iNet Specialist Schools and Academies Trust tda

Student Choice Awards 2008

This Certificate is awarded to

Ms Laditan

In the category of
Best Teacher (F)

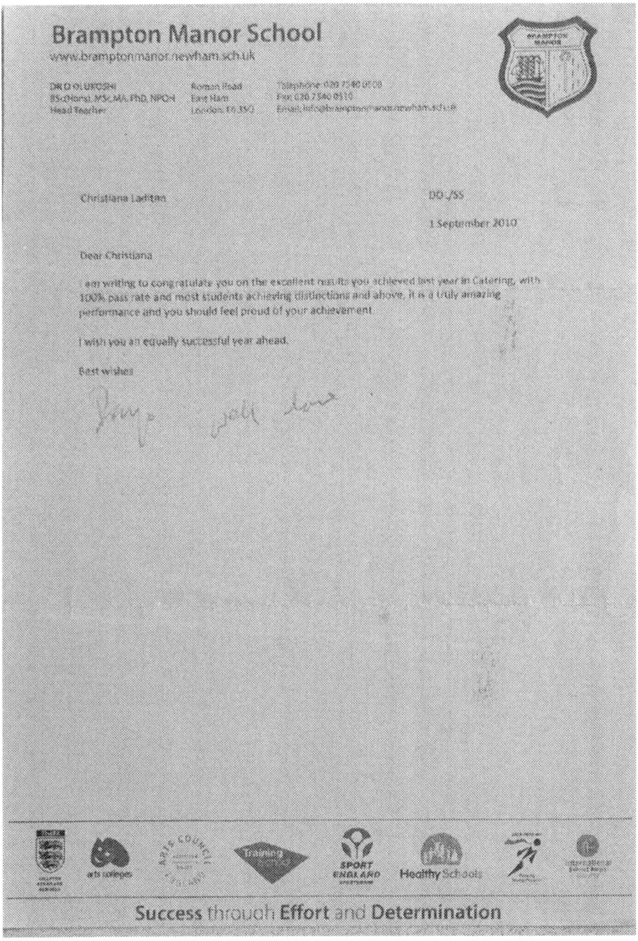

Brampton Manor School
www.bramptonmanor.newham.sch.uk

DR D OLUKOSHI
BSc(Hons), MSc, MA, PhD, NPQH
Head Teacher

Roman Road
East Ham
London E6 3SQ

Telephone: 020 7540 0500
Fax: 020 7540 0510
Email: info@bramptonmanor.newham.sch.uk

Christiana Laditan

DO./SS

1 September 2010

Dear Christiana

I am writing to congratulate you on the excellent results you achieved last year in Catering, with 100% pass rate and most students achieving distinctions and above, it is a truly amazing performance and you should feel proud of your achievement.

I wish you an equally successful year ahead.

Best wishes

arts colleges

Training

SPORT ENGLAND

Healthy Schools

Success through **Effort** and **Determination**

ABOUT THE AUTHOR

Mrs. Christiana Ayodele Laditan Nee Shaw was born at Osogbo in Osun state. Previously old western region. Her parents were Mr and Mrs. Ebenezer Oladunni Shaw. After primary and secondary school in Nigeria, she went United Kingdom to study Home Economics at the University of Liverpool and obtained a Bachelor's degree.

Mrs Laditan is happily married to Mr Folarin Olajide Laditan. They have been happily married for forty-three years. Mrs Laditan is a mother of three children, Mrs Oluwafeyikemi Osinloye, Mr Adeniran Laditan and Mr Akintunde Laditan. She is also blessed with nine grandchildren

Printed in Great Britain
by Amazon

12984458R00077